ALGIRA PEREIRA

7 Shades of Healing

To my mother,
For all the years you carried the burden of worry for me, I hope this book shows you that the past is behind me and I have healed. Now, it's time for you to heal as well. This book is a tribute not only to the healing I've experienced, but to the healing that awaits you and to all those who, like you, have spent their lives carrying the weight of worry. It's time to let go, to find peace, and to heal. I love you, and I want you to know that you, too, embrace your healing Journey.

"The journey to healing isn't about erasing the scars, it's about wearing them as proof of the battles you've survived."

— Algira Pereira

Contents

Take a spoonful of salt and pour it into a glass of water. The water will become sour enough to be consumed, right?

Take the same amount of salt and pour it into a water-filled bucket. The increased quantity of water in the bucket will not affect the water that much, right?

Let's take the same salt and put it in the sea. What will happen? Nothing, right?

Salt in our lives represents our problems, and water quantity is the amount of courage and willpower we hold within. Oftentimes, we underestimate our potential to be a sea. Due to conditioning, many don't even think about being a bucket, let alone becoming the sea.

However, Shifora is the black sheep in this book. Despite starting as a glass, she chooses to become a sea of courage and willpower. Once she reminds herself of her own hidden potential, there is no looking back, and the salt's amount never matters after that.

7 Shades of Healing depicts a rainbow of growth and evolution, which not only happens in Shifora's life after the dark clouds but also stands as a lighthouse of hope to all those who feel lost on their way.

Algira has opened up beyond measure to weave the fragile fabrics of the story into a stunning attire of self-love. After reading it multiple times by now, I am sure it is a magic wand for all those who are awaiting magic in their lives but ignore the fact that they have magic within themselves and can heal themselves.

If only we know…

Heena M Shrivastava

International Book Writing Coach,

Author of 4 books

Seeker of Spiritual Enlightenment.

"Healing is not a destination, it's a journey, often messy, unpredictable, yet transformative."
- Anonymous

When I first envisioned this book, I wanted it to be more than just a story. I wanted it to be a mirror, a reflection of the silent battles we all fight, the pain we carry, and the resilience we discover when we least expect it. At its heart, this novel is a celebration of the human spirit, a testament to the strength it takes to embrace vulnerability and rediscover oneself.

Through the eyes of Shifora, you will walk a path filled with laughter, heartbreak, and moments of introspection. She is flawed yet fearless, broken yet beautiful, a reminder that healing does not demand perfection but authenticity. Her story unfolds in the backdrop of tropical breezes and the salty air of the Maldives, a setting as serene as it is turbulent, mirroring her internal struggles.

This novel is not just about healing, it's about the courage it takes to confront one's past, the grace to forgive oneself, and the determination to move forward despite the scars. It's about the connections we forge, the boundaries we set, and the power of choosing oneself without apology.

Whether you're on your own journey of healing or simply drawn to stories that celebrate life's complexities, I hope this book resonates with you. May Shifora's story inspire you to believe in the possibility of renewal, no matter how broken the pieces may seem.

Take a deep breath, open your heart, and join me in exploring the *7 shades of healing*.

Acknowledgments

To my father, for always encouraging me to pursue my dreams, even when they seemed far beyond reach. Your belief in me has been my greatest motivation.

Thank you Maa for always being there, even when your worry dial was turned up to eleven. Your love and support mean the world, and this book is dedicated to you, for your strength and your ability to be the rock I didn't always realize I needed.

To my Ajju & Reena, thank you for being my constant source of inspiration and for occasionally distracting me just enough to keep my sanity intact. You've inspired every chapter with your stories, whether you knew it or not.

To my close friends, what would I do without you? You've helped me with every little detail, whether it was research, designing, printing, marketing, publishing, or editing (and let's be honest, probably saving me from making some truly questionable decisions). Each of you has contributed in such a unique and important way, from catching the tiniest details

I missed to offering your invaluable advice when I needed it most. There's no way I could've done this without you. You're the real MVPs!

A heartfelt thanks to Heena Shrivastava for your guidance and endless patience, listening to my chaotic ideas, helping me craft this healing journey into a story that actually makes sense, and being the solid support I needed. As I awlays say, your direction have always helped me grow as a better human.

Himani, I thank you for being the first reader and your feedback was invaluable, even when it left me questioning my entire plot (but you were right).

A special thank you to Author Ajay K Pandey, for your direction and wisdom, you've made this process so much easier, one word at a time.

I would also like to express my deepest gratitude to my boss, **Stephane Laguette**, for giving me the incredible opportunity to work with him. This experience was not just a job, it became a turning point in my life. It allowed me an opportunity to reflect on myself, recognize the healing I needed, and embark on this transformative journey. Thank you for being an important part of my story.

And to all of you for reading this book, I hope it inspires you, entertains you, and maybe makes you think a little differently about your own journey. And if it makes you laugh, cry, or wonder what on earth I was thinking, well, that's a bonus.

Lastly, to myself. I actually did it, against all odds, and despite the 3 a.m. writing sessions fueled by caffeine and desperation. I know how stubborn I am.

Thank you all for being a part of this story.

Prologue

Healing is a journey, not a destination.

In the chaos of life's storms, we often lose sight of ourselves. We become tangled in the webs of our past, the memories that haunt us, the doubts that cloud our path. But somewhere, in the quiet moments of reflection, we begin to realize that healing doesn't require perfection, it requires courage. The courage to face our fears, to accept our flaws, and to let go of the weight we've been carrying for far too long.

This book is a story of that very courage. It is not just the story of one woman's healing, but the story of all of us, those who dare to confront their scars and turn them into stories of strength. It's about finding peace in the places we thought were broken, and realizing that sometimes, we need to let go of the past to truly embrace the future.

As you read these pages, know that the journey you're about to take is one of transformation. It may not be easy, and it may not be linear, but with each step, you'll find that the weight begins to lift. You'll find that the pieces of your past are not what define you, they are simply the fuel for the person you are becoming.

This is for everyone who's ever doubted their own strength. For those who've ever felt lost in the maze of their own mind. And most importantly, this is for you, the one who's ready to heal, to rise, and to embrace the beauty of your own story.

Introduction

Life is a journey of healing. It's a process that begins the moment we learn to confront our inner battles and let go of the weight that holds us down. For many of us, that weight comes from the past, the memories, the regrets, the scars of our experiences. We carry them with us like baggage, sometimes unaware of the toll they take on our present. But what if we could free ourselves from this weight? What if we could break free from the chains of our own doubts and fears?

In *7 Shades of Healing*, we follow the story of Shifora, a woman who embarks on a journey of self-healing, a journey that takes her through the ups and downs of love, loss, forgiveness, and ultimately, self-acceptance. Through Shifora's story, we explore the complexities of the human spirit, the process of overcoming self-doubt, and the power of vulnerability in healing. Her journey mirrors the path that many of us must take to find peace and understanding within ourselves.

But this story isn't just about Shifora. It's about all of us. It's about the way we all struggle to reconcile our past with the present and find a way to move forward. It's about learning to embrace our imperfections and understanding that healing is not about becoming perfect, it's about learning to love ourselves despite our flaws.

Through her relationship with Sid, her closest friends, and even the people she meets along the way, Shifora learns that healing doesn't happen in isolation. It happens when we allow ourselves to be vulnerable, to connect with others, and to trust the process. Along the way, she discovers that true healing lies in the power of self-love, forgiveness, and the courage to let go.

This book is not just a story it's a reminder. A reminder that no matter how dark or painful our past may seem, there is always hope for a brighter future. A future where we are free to be who we truly are, without the weight of past mistakes or regrets holding us back. It's a story for anyone who has ever felt broken, lost, or unsure. It's for those who are ready to take the first step toward healing, no matter how daunting it may seem.

As you turn these pages, may you find the courage to heal, to grow, and to embrace the beautiful person you are becoming. This is the beginning of your own journey, your own 7 Shades of Healing.

One

The Interrupted Introduction

"Tring, Tring"

'The shrill sound of her phone pierced through the hushed atmosphere of the meeting room. All eyes turned towards Shifora, who stood at the head of the long mahogany table, mid-presentation. Her hand flew to her pocket, hastily silencing the device, but the damage was done. The rhythm of her carefully rehearsed words had been broken, and the tension in the room was palpable.

Shifora's boss, Mr. Kapoor, sat at the opposite end, his brow furrowed in evident disapproval. The client representatives shifted uncomfortably in their seats, exchanging subtle glances. Shifora's cheeks flushed with embarrassment as she attempted a quick recovery, throwing out a nervous laugh and a hurried apology.

"I'm sorry about that," Shifora said, *her voice tight with nerves.* "Please continue." Mr. Kapoor voiced out from the side.

When Shifora finally concluded, she glanced uneasily at Mr. Kapoor, Steeling herself for the upcoming reprimanding she assumed.

To her surprise, Mr. Kapoor's expression softened

slightly. "Shifora, excellent job on the presentation," he said, his tone more approving than she had anticipated. "You managed to turn things around after that interruption." Shifora let out a breath she hadn't realized she was holding. "Thank you, sir," she replied,

Mr. Kapoor leaned forward, his gaze penetrating. "However, about that phone ……" he continued, his voice dropping to a serious tone., "That's not something we can afford to overlook. Make sure it doesn't happen again."

Shifora felt a flush of embarrassment creep up her neck. Shifora nodded. "Of all the mistakes, why did it have to be something so avoidable?" She knew she was better than this. As Mr. Kapoor's words lingered in the air, her mind raced through a dozen excuses, but she held them back. This was not the time for justifications, only resolve. Keep it together, Shifora, she thought, forcing a calm nod in response. "Don't let this slip-up define you."

After concluding the meeting, Shifora dropped one of the clients off at their hotel on her way home. She was so lost in her thoughts, that she did not realize when she even got out of the taxi and was standing inside her building in front of the elevator.

"Beep beep…" Her phone buzzed, as if it couldn't wait to interrupt. It was then that she remembered the disruption in the meeting, the phone call that had nearly cost her the presentation. With a sinking feeling, she realized she hadn't checked her phone since the incident. She reached into her bag and pulled it out, half-expecting to find a missed call & a message from Sid. Shifora's heart sank as she read the message.

"See you at the café in 30 minutes," Sid's message read. Classic Sid is always straight to the point, just like he'd always been. No fluff, no elaboration. Shifora blithe faintly at the memory of how she used to crave those deeper, face-to-face conversations, the kind that lingered on long after the words had been spoken. But Sid? He was never one for that. He preferred the efficiency of one-liners, leaving the rest unsaid, unspoken, yet somehow always understood.

She cursed under her breath. How could she have forgotten? The reminder had slipped her mind entirely amidst the chaos of the day. She glanced at the time. There were only 15 minutes left before the meeting, and THE COFFEE CLUB was just 5 minutes away from her residence.

Her mind and heart began playing see-saw. Heart whispered to cancel this meeting once again, but mind asked-'till how long?' Despite her guarded heart, she feared the old, unresolved question Sid had posed years ago. She knew it wasn't just a matter of words, Sid's eyes had a way of asking questions that words never could. She felt an irresistible pull towards him, a magnetic connection she couldn't ignore, stirring a long-forgotten hope for something more.

She stared at the blurring letters on her phone, tears welling up. With a deep breath, she typed out a response. "Hi Sid, I've been thinking a lot, and I realize I've been avoiding this for too long. But enough is enough. Yes, I'll be there. It's time to stop dodging and catch up. See you soon!"

As soon as she entered her apartment, she slipped out of her simple yet elegant brown Kolhapuri sandals, the familiar click of the door echoing in the quiet room. She placed her office laptop on the sofa, her mind preoccupied with the upcoming meeting. Heading to the kitchen, she filled the kettle, and the rhythmic sound of boiling water offered little comfort.

She glanced at herself in the mirror, the reflection of the beige saree she wore adding a touch of elegance to her otherwise tense demeanor. With a sip of warm water, she allowed herself a brief moment of calm before changing into a flowing long cotton dress in vibrant shades of turquoise and coral light and airy, a stark contrast to her nerves.

As she grabbed her keys and wallet and slung a large woven tote bag over her shoulder, her phone buzzed with a message that made her pause. A glance revealed a cryptic text, "I have reached." With a deep breath, she stepped out and walked down the lane to the café, the weight of anticipation heavy in her chest. The familiar street felt different tonight as if it was holding its breath.'

Two

Reunion at The Coffee Club

'As Shifora stepped into the café, she darted through the space, her gaze scanning the sea-blue wooden chairs adorned with matching cushions that added a touch of coastal charm to the interior. The chairs were positioned around sleek, polished wooden tables that gleamed under the soft glow of overhead sea glass pendant lights. Each table was set with minimalist white ceramic mugs and saucers, ready for the next round of customers.

The walls of the café were painted a soothing pale turquoise, reminiscent of the shallow waters near the shore. Hanging on these walls were paintings that depicted scenes of Maldivian life, vivid coral reefs teeming with tropical fish, serene lagoons with overwater bungalows, and golden sunsets over the Indian Ocean. One painting caught Shifora's eye: a lone sailboat drifting on a tranquil azure sea, the setting sun casting a warm orange glow over the horizon. It reminded her of the chaos

10

that had settled from her life, and her mind was glowing like a sunset.

The cushions on the chairs were a mix of sea blues and sandy neutrals, adorned with embroidered seashells and palm fronds, adding to the coastal aesthetic. A woven rattan partition stood near the entrance, adorned with seagrass baskets filled with vibrant tropical flowers hibiscus, bougainvillea, and frangipani, adding bursts of red, pink, and yellow to the serene surroundings. The café's cutlery, though simple, had a polished silver finish that gleamed softly in the natural light filtering through large windows overlooking the ocean.

As Shifora made her way deeper into the café, her senses were hit with the aroma of freshly brewed coffee mingled with the salty tang of the sea breeze, creating an intoxicating blend that stirred something deep within her. *It was the kind of place that invited you to stay, to linger,* Shifora thought.

Her eyes scanned the room until they settled on a tall figure occupying a corner table. He had well-trimmed, short brown hair and fair skin. A Tahitian tattoo adorned his right arm, proudly displayed by his white sleeveless shirt. His ensemble was complete with loose military trousers and a pair of rugged Woodland shoes. *What an overpowering personality,* she thought to herself, feeling a twinge of nervousness. It was Sid, of course!

As she approached the table, Sid looked up, his face breaking into a casual smile. "Hey, Shifora," he greeted, his tone as relaxed as ever. There was no hint of the tension she was feeling. *Typical Sid,* she thought. *Always unbothered, always in control.*

"Hey," she replied, trying to match his nonchalance but failing to mask the undercurrent of emotions swirling within her.

As they sat across from each other, the silence between them stretched, thick with unspoken words. Shifora wrapped her hands around her glass of water, staring into the transparent liquid as if it held the answers. *What am I supposed to say?* she wondered. Should I tell him the truth, or should I make up some story? Will he judge me? She glanced up at Sid, his gaze fixed on the table, seemingly lost in thought.

What's she thinking? Sid wondered. He could feel the tension in the air, the weight of everything they weren't saying. *I wish I could just ask her, but what if it opens old wounds that I am not aware of?* Sid mused.

Meanwhile, Shifora's thoughts swirled. *Is he still the same? Did he find someone?* The café around them buzzed with life, but at that moment, they were both trapped in their minds, caught between the past and the unspoken present.

The 90's melodies playing softly in the background, a medley of Shahrukh Khan's iconic songs, seemed to carry a weight of nostalgia, memories of a time when life felt simpler when their paths hadn't yet diverged so dramatically. *"Tujhe Dekha Toh Ye .... Sanam..."* filled the air, bringing with it echoes of love.'

Three

Sid's Flashback

'Sid was excited, lost in nostalgia about how he met Shifora in their college days, how he fell in love with her, and how he still feels about her.

Their friendship dates back to their college days, a time filled with youthful energy and ambition. They had met during an NCC camp in Nagaland, India. Sid in his NCC uniform was a picture of discipline and authority. The crisp olive-green fabric hugged his frame, accentuating his athletic build. The neatly ironed shirt bore the insignia of the 7 Delhi Battalion, and his beret sat perfectly on his head, with the badge gleaming under the sunlight. His dark hair was always neatly trimmed, and his sharp jawline gave him an air of seriousness and determination. Sid's eyes, focused and piercing, reflected his commitment to his duties. His polished boots, which he kept immaculate, echoed his meticulous nature.

Shifora, in her uniform, was the embodiment of grace and strength. The uniform fit her perfectly, highlighting her slender yet strong physique. The 1 Goa Girls Battalion badge was proudly displayed on her arm, a symbol which she was proud of. Her beret, slightly tilted, added a touch of fierceness to her look. Shifora's long, dark hair was usually pulled back into a tight bun, emphasizing her sharp cheekbones and expressive eyes. Her eyes, filled with determination and a hint of warmth, always seemed to be on the lookout for the next challenge. The way she carried herself, with an effortless blend of elegance and authority, made her stand out.

Her competitive nature drove her to excel, and it was this very quality that had initially sparked a friendly rivalry between her and Sid.

In those days, the NCC camps were a blend of rigorous training and camaraderie. Sid and Shifora often found themselves pitted against each other in various activities, from obstacle courses to tactical drills.

One day it was a grueling obstacle course. The cadets lined up at the starting point, the atmosphere thick with competitive energy. Sid's and Shifora's eyes met briefly, a spark of rivalry passing between them.

A whistle blew, and they were off. Sid's team moved like a well-oiled machine, each member playing their part to perfection. They scaled walls, crawled under nets, and leaped over hurdles with precision. Sid led by example, his athleticism and strategic thinking shining through as he navigated the course with ease.

Shifora's team, however, was not to be underestimated. They tackled each obstacle with fierce determination, their camaraderie evident in the way they supported one another.

Shifora's agility and quick thinking were impressive, and she inspired her team to push beyond their limits.

As they reached the final stretch, the competition grew even more intense. Both teams were neck and neck, the finish line just a few meters away. Sid and Shifora, leading their respective teams, sprinted with everything they had.

In the final moment, Shifora's teammate stumbled, but she quickly helped her up, sacrificing precious seconds. Sid noticed this and urged his team to give one final push. They crossed the finish line just moments before Shifora's team.

The field erupted in cheers and applause.

Sid walked over to Shifora, extending his hand with a genuine smile. "Great effort, Shifora. You and your team were incredible."

Shifora shook his hand, a determined glint in her eye. "Thanks, Sid. Your team deserved the win. But don't get too comfortable, we'll be coming for you next time."

Sid chortled, appreciating her competitive spirit. "I wouldn't expect anything less."

Four

Confessions of the Heart

"We are hardwired to connect with others, and the time we spend together, whether at work, on a project, or during a fleeting moment, creates bonds that often run deeper than we realize. In those shared experiences, we find pieces of ourselves reflected, and that's where attachment begins."
... Ref ..Social: Why Our Brains Are Wired to Connect is a book by Matthew D. Lieberman.

'NCC participants have the chance to attend camps lasting 8, 15, or 21 days, organized periodically over the 3-5 years of their training program. These camps provide immersive experiences that build resilience, leadership, and camaraderie among cadets.

After completing a series of camps together from 2005 to 2007, a natural closeness developed between them. The shared experiences had woven their lives together in ways they hadn't fully grasped at the time. But ever since returning from the NCC camp in Nagaland, he had felt an inexplicable emptiness, as if a piece of his heart had been left behind. It was in those moments of connection, forged through time and shared challenges, that attachment had quietly taken root, leaving a void when they were apart.

Sid sat alone in his apartment, the dim light from his desk lamp casting long shadows on the wall. He stared at the pile of books in front of him, but his mind was elsewhere. The memories of those days flooded his mind. He vividly remembered the first time he had truly noticed Shifora, not just as a fellow cadet, but as someone special. It was during a quiet evening at the camp. They were all gathered around a bonfire, sharing stories and laughs. Shifora's laughter was infectious, her eyes sparkling with joy as she animatedly narrated an incident from her childhood. Sid found himself drawn to her, captivated by her spirit and the way she seemed to light up the entire gathering. At that moment, he realized that something in his life had shifted, a quiet recognition that his world was a little brighter with her in it.

As the days passed, he observed her more closely. Her leadership qualities were admirable, but it was her kindness and the way she encouraged her team that touched him the most.

Once Sid watched from a distance as Shifora stood beside a young cadet, his face red with frustration as he struggled to complete the drill. The rest of the group had already moved on, but Shifora stayed behind, her voice steady and calm. "You've got this," she encouraged, demonstrating the movement again, slower this time. The cadet's hands shook, but Shifora remained patient, guiding him through each step with a quiet determination. When he stumbled, she caught him, offering a reassuring smile. "Try again. You're almost there."

After several more attempts, the cadet finally nailed the drill, his eyes lighting up with triumph. Shifora clapped him on the shoulder, her own face breaking into a proud smile. "See? I knew you could do it." Sid couldn't help but admire the way she handled the situation, how she refused to give up on the cadet, pushing him to his limits while still showing her support. It was moments like these that made him realize just how determined and compassionate she was, always pushing herself and those around her to be their best.

————-

Back in Delhi, Sid couldn't shake off these thoughts. His friends noticed the change in him. "You've got it bad, haven't you?" one of his friends teased as they sat in their favorite café. Sid just gratified, knowing it was true. Shifora had become a constant presence in his thoughts, and he couldn't help but miss her.

Determined to stay connected, he started sending her little surprises. Through his network of long-distance friends, he managed to arrange for flowers, chocolates, and even her favorite ice cream to be delivered to her. He remembered her love for Panipuri and enlisted the help of a local friend to send a fresh batch to her doorstep. Each time, he received a message of thanks from her, and it warmed his heart to know that he could bring a smile to her face, even from miles away.

His friends, who had become his partners in crime for the surprises, encouraged him to confess his feelings. "You've got to tell her, Sid. You can't keep this to yourself forever," one of them said. "Let's plan a reunion," said another. "yayaaya, Goa it is" others chorused. They all had planned a reunion of the NCC Nagaland batch. They all met at Miramar Beach in Panjim.

———-

At Miramar Beach Panjim - Goa

As they sat down, Sid's heart pounded in his chest. He took a deep breath and looked into her eyes. "Shifora, there's something I need to tell you," he began, his voice steady despite the storm of emotions inside him. "I've fallen in love with you. I can't stop thinking about you, and I miss you every single day."

Shifora's eyes widened in surprise, and for a moment, there was silence. Sid could see the conflict in her eyes. She finally spoke, her voice soft but firm.

Shifora playfully patted Sid on the shoulder and said, "Oh, come on, Sid! don't be such a wimp. I thought you were the strong, tough guy who wouldn't fall for all those Bollywood clichés. Look, I don't know about you, but I've got big plans for my future, and I have no clue where they're taking me. I don't want to jump into something where I can't keep my word. So, let's drop the whole Shahrukh Khan act, and both of us can focus on our dream of joining the army, okay?"

Sid grinned and gave Shifora a mock salute. "Aye aye, Captain! I'll trade my Shahrukh Khan dreams for some serious study time. But just so you know, if you ever need a Bollywood backup dancer for your army plans, you know where to find me. And hey, don't worry "I'll keep my wimpiness in check while you chase those big dreams!". Shifora didn't realize just how those words had hurt Sid, and Sid at that time could have won an Oscar for his performance, as his smile did not reveal the hurt that Shifora's dismissal of his feelings had caused.

Shifora went to her friends, Lalita dragged her aside, and having eavesdropped on their conversation, burst in with a dramatic flair. "Shifora, seriously? I know you're into him too, why are you being so ridiculous? Don't turn down a chance with a total heartthrob like that! Go for it! If you break his heart, I swear I'll track you down and break yours!"

Shifora, tears welling up, took a shaky breath before replying, "Lalita, it's not that simple. Please, don't tell him anything.

I've got responsibilities right now. Even if I manage to come to the camps and hang out with you guys, being the eldest, my family comes first. We're in our final year, and right now, all that matters is finding a job to support my family since my dad is out of work. I'm not even sure about the army yet, securing a job is my top priority. If I say yes to Sid, I'd just pull him into these challenges. I want him to focus on his dreams, not get caught up in my mess."

Five

The Search

"*Sometimes, the hardest part of finding someone is realizing they've been a part of your journey all along. It's like searching for a lost chapter in a book you've read a thousand times, only to discover the story was incomplete without it.*"............
....Algira Pereira

'After graduation, life took Sid and Shifora on different paths. They moved on, each chasing their dreams and ambitions.

Sid searched for Shifora everywhere. He asked his friends about her and asked her friends about Shifora. No one knew where she was, and no one had her contacts. He was going crazy missing her and not being able to hear from her. It was as if she had vanished, leaving a gaping hole in his life.

9 years passed, each day a little duller without the spark of Shifora's presence in Sid's life. He buried himself in work, trying to move on, but there was always a part of him that missed her.

Tanya had recently become friends with Sid on Facebook through a mutual acquaintance. One evening, as Sid mindlessly scrolled through his feed, a post from Tanya caught his eye. It was a wedding photo, and at the center of the celebration was Shifora, radiant in her bridal attire, the caption read "Shifora weds Arif". Sid's heart tremble, hiis vision blurred as tears welled up, and a raw, primal scream threatened to escape his throat. The pain was unbearable, like a vice tightening around his chest.

Days passed in a haze of torment. Sid replayed the image over and over in his mind, each time feeling a fresh stab of agony. Then, one day, the post vanished. Desperate for answers, Sid reached out to Tanya, the girl who had posted the photo. With a mixture of dread and hope, he asked about Shifora's whereabouts. Tanya revealed that Shifora had married a Maldivian and was now settled in the Maldives, "she had asked me to take down her marriage photos from Facebook, I didn't ask her why since it is her personal choice." Sid remembered Tanya's words

Sid's heart sank. It felt as though the ground had slipped from beneath his feet. He thought he had lost Shifora for good, and the realization was a bitter pill to swallow. The weight of it pressed down on him, making it hard to breathe.

Sid couldn't shake the feeling that something was incomplete. The image of Shifora in her wedding dress haunted his every thought. He had to see her, to talk to her one last time. Driven by this need, Sid began searching for her again. He scoured every social media platform, leaving no stone unturned in his quest to reconnect. He left messages with Tanya, hoping for some hint or lead.

"Tanya, please. Anything? Do you know if she's active anywhere else? Instagram, Twitter, anything?" Sid's voice was edged with desperation during one of their late-night calls.

"I'm sorry, Sid," Tanya replied sympathetically. "I haven't heard from her in a while. Last I knew, she was happy in Maldives, but she seems to have disappeared online."

Sid felt a heavy weight settle on his chest. It seemed like

Shifora had completely forgotten him. Yet, his resolve only grew stronger. He applied for various jobs in the Maldives, thinking that being there in person might give him a better chance to find her.

"I need to do this," Sid whispered to himself one night, staring at the ceiling of his darkened room. "I need closure, for my peace."

Six

The Search Continues

'Despite his efforts, no opportunities came his way. Days turned into weeks, and weeks into months, but still no luck for years. Sid's determination never wavered. His skills, honed during his NCC days, caught the attention of one of his seniors, now a successful entrepreneur. In 2021, this senior reached out to Sid with a job offer.

Sid was pacing in his room when his phone rang. Seeing the familiar name flash on the screen, he quickly answered.

"Hello, Sid? This is Rohit from NCC," came the familiar voice. "I heard you're looking for a job in the Maldives. I have a position that might interest you."

Sid's heart leaped. "Rohit, it's great to hear from you! Yes, I've been trying to get to the Maldives. I have… personal reasons."

Rohit giggled, "I figured as much. We need someone with

leadership skills. It's a challenging role, but I think you're up for it."

Sid's mind raced. This was the break he had been waiting for. "Thank you, Rohit. You have no idea how much this means to me. I won't let you down."

That night, Sid lay in bed, a mix of hope and anxiety churning within him. "This is it," he thought. "I'll find her. I have to."

In the weeks that followed, Sid prepared for his move. He packed his bags with a sense of purpose, his thoughts never straying far from Shifora. He could almost see her, hear her laughter, feel the unfinished business between them. This reminds me of that song from the Salman Khan movie *Pyaar Kiya Toh Darna Kya* — "Deewana Mein Chala." (*Why Fear When in Love* — "I Wander, Crazy in Love.")

As the plane descended over the azure waters of the Maldives, Sid's heart pounded with anticipation. He whispered to himself, "I'm coming, Shifora. This time, I won't give up until I find you." Sid said it out loud to himself.

—————-

The café - Gloria Jeans, where Sid Joined as a team leader nestled by the pristine beaches of the Maldives, was a bustling spot known for its vibrant ambiance and delicious food. Sid quickly adapted to his new role, his natural abilities making him a valuable asset to the team. He enjoyed the work, but there was always a lingering sense of incompleteness.

Sid's search for Shifora was relentless and filled with hope, even amidst the vastness of the Maldives. He began his search during his breaks and off-shift hours, by waiting outside the State Bank of India, the only main branch for expat Indians in the capital city of Malé, assuming she might come there sometimes. Each day, of course during the off hours, he stood there, scanning the faces of those who entered and left, hoping to catch a glimpse of her. In the evenings, he waited outside ATMs, thinking she might need to withdraw cash. His heart skipped a beat every time someone approached, only to sink again when it wasn't her.

Determined, he spent his free time at the library, flipping through books and keeping an eye on the entrance, just in case she might walk in. He wandered through parks and gardens, hoping to see her among the crowds. His eyes constantly searched, but she remained elusive. Malé is a small city, Sid didn't even know if Shifora lived in Resort, local island, or Malé. But He had high hopes that he would spot Shifora at least once in Malé' being the main hub for everything.

His desperation grew, and he started mentioning his search to his regular customers at the restaurant where he worked. "I'm looking for an old friend," he would say, showing them an old photo of Shifora. "Have you seen her around?"

The responses were always the same, a shake of the head, a sympathetic smile. "Sorry, I haven't seen her," they would say. But Sid never gave up. He knew he had to keep searching, to leave no stone unturned. Each day, he pushed forward, driven by the hope that one day, he would find her.'

Seven

The Miracle it is

Year 2022

'Despite the years that had passed, his feelings for her remained strong. His past efforts had come to naught, but he wasn't ready to give up. The digital age had brought with it new tools, and Sid turned to Instagram, where he had spent hours in search of Shifora.

After a few months of searches on social media and sifting through countless profiles, his heart skipped a beat when he found a profile that matched Shifora's name and face. He was ecstatic, this time, the search had clicked. She was finally on Instagram, Sid Jumped out of bed in excitement, his eyes full of tears and fingers trembling. Sid sent her a message with a mix of excitement and apprehension.

"Hi Shifora, it's Sid from the NCC camp days. Long time no see! I hope you're doing well."

A day passed, then another, with no reply. Sid tried not to read too much into it—people get busy, he told himself. But when her response finally came, it was a simple, almost curt message.

"Hi, Sid. Yes, it's been a while. I'm doing fine, thanks for reaching out."

Sid enrapt as he read her message, but something felt off. He chalked it up to time, years of distance, perhaps. He replied with a joke, trying to recapture the easy chats they once shared.

But her reply was delayed again, and when it came, it was polite but formal.

Their conversation continued in the same vein, exchanges about the weather & work. Sid Normally talks straightforwardly, but out of excitement found himself typing out long messages, filled with nostalgia and questions, but her replies were shorter, more reserved.

At first, Sid dismissed the feeling of unease. He thought she might just be busy or distracted. But as days turned into weeks, the pattern persisted. There was a hesitation in her words, a distance that hadn't been there before. The vibrant, carefree Shifora he remembered seemed replaced by someone guarded, almost cautious.

Sid's excitement slowly morphed into something else, uncertainty, maybe even sadness. The warmth of their old friendship felt like it was slipping through his fingers, replaced by something more like small talk between acquaintances.

Their conversations were stilted, filled with polite exchanges but lacking the warmth and familiarity that once defined their friendship. Sid felt a pang of sadness as he realized that Shifora was not the same person he remembered. There was a distance in her responses and the connection they once had seemed to be slipping away. He began to wonder what had changed in Shifora's life, and if he'd ever truly know.

Determined to understand what had changed, Sid decided he needed to see her in person. He had heard from a mutual friend that Shifora was married now, which added another layer of complexity to his feelings. Despite knowing this, Sid wanted to hear everything from her lips. He wanted to know how her life had unfolded, what dreams she had pursued, and how she had changed over the years. Why Marriage? How?

Sid sent another message, suggesting they meet up if she was comfortable with it.

Shifora replied politely but distantly, "Hi Sid, I appreciate your offer, but I'm quite busy this weekend. Perhaps another time."

Sid had felt a bit disappointed but replied, "Sure, no problem. Let me know whenever you're free."

A few weeks later, Sid had tried again. "Hey Shifora, I'm going to that art exhibition this Friday. Would you like to come with me?"

Shifora replied, "Hi Sid, thanks for the invite, but I have other plans on Friday. Maybe next time."

Sid had sensed her reluctance but replied, "Okay, no worries. Let me know when you're free."

Despite these attempts, Shifora always seemed to find a reason not to meet Sid in person. He couldn't help but feel a bit puzzled and frustrated. He admired her professionalism but the more she denied it, the stronger his urge to meet her.

After several failed attempts for 2 years, Shifora agreed. They decided to meet at a cozy café, THE COFFEE CLUB.

The years have changed many things. Shifora now seemed quite sophisticated in her demeanor, more mature, and she stuck to the point during their chats, avoiding the playful tangents they once enjoyed. Yet, beneath the surface of their more measured conversations, there was still a familiarity, a shared history that neither time nor distance could erase.

He was cheery, recalling the countless times they had pushed each other to be better, both in the camps and in life. Watching her now, Sid couldn't help but admire how confident and self-dependent she had become.'

Eight

The Angel has arrived

At cafe...

'Shifora cleared her throat. Sid's thoughts were interrupted. As their eyes met, a flicker of uncertainty danced across his features. His smile was slightly constricted as he struggled to find the right words.

As an uncomfortable silence settled between them, Shifora sought to bridge the gap with a simple gesture of hospitality. "Would you like to have tea or coffee?" she offered, her voice gentle and inviting.

Sid, despite his bold nature, felt a flicker of nervousness but masked it with a confident smile. "I'll take a coffee, thanks. And maybe some company with that?" he replied, his eyes twinkling mischievously.

Shifora appreciating his playful tone. "Coffee it is, and since you asked so nicely, I suppose I can join you," she teased back, heading to the counter.

Shifora placed an order at the counter and returned to the seat, " So Sid, what are you doing in Maldives?"

Sid shrugged his shoulders and said. "Well, I was searching for you!"

Shifora grinned "You know if you keep this up, people might start thinking you're my private investigator! What's the scoop, did you finally find me in the 'Missing Persons' column?"

"Not really" Sid reacted, but at least "apna persons column" (our people column).

Shifora guffawed.

"What brought you to Maldives? You had different dreams isn't it?" Sid Investigated

Shifora delighted, enjoying the sweet talks. "Well, plans change as we grow, life takes us to the path the universe has assigned us to. Anyways, that's past. I work as a Business Analyst. My job involves a lot of fieldwork and research, which I love.

Sid's eyes lit up. "A Business Analyst? That's amazing. No wonder you look so refined like a business woman now"

"NOW? What do you mean? Did'nt I look ——- in NCC days?" makes a face. Then let her only laugh it off as he coughs nervously. "Ok, Baksh dia. (I have forgiven you) Enough about me," Sid responded. How long have you been in Malé? What's it like living here?" Sid's questions were casual, but Shifora knew exactly what he was getting at. She looked at him with a knowing gaze, her eyes wide with wonder.

Sid leaned forward, intrigued. "And will you introduce me to your husband?" he asked, his interest sparked.

Shifora shrugged casually. "Who knows? Maybe when pigs fly!" Enjoying this light-hearted conversation.

Sid grinned, appreciating her sense of humor. "Well, I'll be on the lookout for flying pigs then…." he replied, matching her playful tone.

Their playful chatter gradually faded into a comfortable silence as they both sipped their coffee, lost in their thoughts. Shifora gazed out of the café window, watching the gentle sway of palm trees in the ocean breeze.

Sid cleared his throat, breaking the silence. "but seriously! I want to know your story. How did you meet your husband?" he asked, his tone softening with genuine interest. The question hung in the air, pregnant with the deep jealousy behind the questioning. I want to know everything about you Shifora, how did you get to the person you are today?"

Shifora set down her cup, her expression becoming more contemplative. After this, she became quiet, as if collecting her courage, thought by thought. And Sid held the space for her as if waiting to be drenched in her thoughts.

Shifora had encountered this question multiple times in the past, whether in intimate conversations with friends and family, in the courtroom during registrations, in the church for nuptials, and even in the Bishop House during statement procedures. Despite the familiarity of this question, it always felt like someone sprayed salt on her wounds, familiar yet stinging.

Each time, it brought back a flood of memories, both sweet and painful. She had learned to navigate these inquiries with a calm exterior, but inside, it always churned up a storm of emotions. Shifora looked at Sid, who was watching her with a mix of questions and concern and she decided to be honest.

She had already climbed the mountain and now it was time to come downhill. It may look smoother, but only she knew that these 10 years of journey would snowball into another mountain of emotions.'

Nine

Fish Out of Water

"Calm down, Shifora, you've got this," I muttered, gripping my pink flashy carry-on bag too tightly. My palms were sweaty, and I could feel my heart pounding in my chest. "It's just an airport. People do this every day. Even if it is your first international trip and you've got every right to be a bundle of nerves."

Unfortunately, my pep talk didn't seem to help. I bumped into the first person I encountered, nearly toppling over his luggage cart. "Sorry! Sorry!" I exclaimed, trying to steady myself. The man gave me a bemused look before moving on.

"Great start, Shifora," I grumbled under my breath. As I made my way to the customs area, I tried to calm my racing thoughts. "Okay, deep breaths. Just need to get through customs and then find my luggage."

Approaching the Customs Officer, I handed over my passport with shaky hands. The officer glanced at it, then back at me. "Ma'am, this is your boarding pass."

"Oh! right, sorry," I said, feeling my face flush with embarrassment. I fumbled through my bag, finally finding my passport and handing it over. The officer's eyebrows raised slightly, but he processed it without comment.

"Just keep it together, Shifora," I whispered as I walked away, ignoring the curious glances of nearby travelers. I was practically radiating awkwardness.

As I made my way to baggage claim, I couldn't help but replay the flight time. Thankfully, I had managed to temporarily quell my anxiety during the flight thanks to Seem, a co-passenger. A cheerful woman in her late thirties who was visiting the Maldives for a vacation.

I had boarded the plane in panic, my mind swirling with worries about my new job, living in a new country, and whether I was making the right choice.

Taking a deep breath, I tried to open the water bottle. Just then, the water spilled. Mujhe toh thik se khana bhi nahi ata, (I don't even know how to eat properly) what if they laugh at me? What if they laugh at what I wear? This is my first time traveling abroad. What if the climate doesn't suit me? What if I don't like the place? I even bought clothes just for a month. If I don't like the job and place, I will run home. Waise bhi mei, NCC cadet reh chuki hoo, (anyway, I have been an NCC Cadet) I am not afraid to travel.

As I buckled my seatbelt, I noticed the woman sitting next to me was already flipping through a glossy travel magazine. She had an air of confidence about her, the kind that comes from frequent travels. She caught my eye and charmed.

"First time in the Maldives?" she asked, her voice melodic and reassuring.

"Is it that obvious?" I replied, feeling a mix of excitement and nervousness. "I'm Shifora, by the way."

"Seema," she said, extending her hand. "And yes, it's a bit obvious. You have that 'first adventure' glow. Don't worry, I was the same on my first trip here. Now, I come so often, they might as well name an island after me."

I was pleased, grateful for her humor. "What keeps bringing you back?"

"Where do I start? The turquoise waters, the vibrant marine life, the way the sunsets paint the sky… It's like nature decided to show off a little extra here," she said, her eyes twinkling. "What about you? What's your story?"

"I got a job as a Front Office Associate at one of the resorts," I said, my excitement bubbling over. "It's my first time working abroad."

"That's fantastic!" Seema exclaimed. "You're going to love it. The Maldives has this way of making you feel like you're living in a dream. Any worries about the job?"

"A few," I admitted. "I'm excited, but I'm also nervous about adjusting to a new culture and being away from home."

"Totally understandable," Seema said, nodding. "But here's a tip, **Embrace everything**. The locals, the food, the traditions. And don't be afraid to ask questions. You'd be surprised how much people appreciate true wonder."

"Sounds amazing," I said, making a mental note. "Any weird customs I should know about?"

Seema grinned. "Well, if you ever get invited to a local home, be prepared to eat with your hands. And don't be surprised if you're offered a lot of fish. Maldivians love their seafood. Just smile, eat, and enjoy. Oh, and try not to get sunburned on your first day. It's a rookie mistake."

"I'll do my best," I said, smiling. "Any hidden gems I should explore?"

"Visit some of the lesser-known islands, and if you get a chance, go snorkeling or diving. The underwater world here is like something out of a fairy tale. Oh, and take a sunset cruise. There's nothing like it," she said dreamily.

"Thanks, Seema," I said, feeling more at ease.

"I was feeling a bit more relaxed. We chatted for the rest of the flight, Seema sharing her travel tips and funny anecdotes, and me soaking up every bit of information. By the time we started our descent, I felt more excited than nervous, ready to embrace whatever the Maldives had in store for me."

Ten

The First Step in THE MALDIVES

"Hey! That's my suitcase!" a tall, imposing man with a scowl that could curdle milk, yanked my suitcase away from me.

The bag looked like a forlorn puppy, its handle drooping in resignation, I squinted at the luggage tag. "Sorry, but this is my suitcase.

The man glared at me. "I don't think so. This one's mine. I've been waiting for this bag for ages!"

"The tag says 'Shifora,' and unless your name is Shifora, I think you've got the wrong bag." I said.

The man huffed, looking even more irritated. "Well, it's got the same color and brand as mine. Maybe your tag is wrong."

I rolled my eyes. "Or maybe you're just having a really bad day. I'm telling you, this is my bag."

Just then, an airport employee, sensing the rising tension, intervened. "Is there a problem here?"

Before I could respond, the man blurted out, "She's claiming my suitcase is hers!"

"Arey, andhe ho kya? Mera naam nahi dikh raha tumhe? (Are you blind? don't you see my name there?)" I thought it out loud.

The employee looked at both of us, then at the luggage tags, and sighed. "Okay, let's see. Miss Shifora, this is your bag," he said, pointing to the tag on the suitcase I was holding. "And sir, here's your bag," he continued, gesturing to the identical suitcase next to it. "They have different tags, so I suggest you double-check."

The man's face flushed with embarrassment as he grudgingly switched to his suitcase. "My bad, Guess I was in the wrong."

"Haan, bilkul?" (of course) - my mind spoke out aloud again. I gave him a wry smile. "Don't worry about it. At least we're not missing our luggage now."

With the suitcase saga resolved, I headed for the exit, muttering to myself, "If this is how my day's starting, I'm in for a real adventure."

Stepping outside, the reality of my new life felt like a gentle nudge rather than a wave. The vibrant colors of the island, the lush greenery, and the crystal-clear waters seemed like a promise of the adventures to come.

"Alright, Shifora," I murmured, trying to lift my spirits, "this is the start of something amazing. You can do this."

Back then, I wore navy blue jeans, a red t-shirt adorned with a small smiley in the corner, and black sneakers, my sense of fashion was, well, nonexistent. As I trudged towards the taxi stand, Ali, my island guide and soon-to-be friend, turned to me with a grin that hinted at future mischief.

As we walked towards the taxi stand, Ali turned to me with a grin. "So, Shifora, are you ready to become an islander? First lesson, always smile. It's the Maldivian way."

I couldn't help but laugh. "I'll do my best, Ali. Tell me, what's the most important thing I need to know about living here?"

"Well," Ali said, pretending to think hard, "always have a backup plan for your sandals. They have a habit of disappearing at the beach."

"Noted," I replied, chuckling. "And what about the job at the resort? What should I expect as a front office associate?"

"Oh, it's a mix of serious hospitality and fun in the sun. We work hard to ensure our guests are happy, but we also know how to enjoy ourselves. And if you ever feel overwhelmed, just remember, you're surrounded by the most beautiful ocean in the world. It's hard to stay stressed when you can just dive in."

His easygoing nature made the transition so much smoother. I found myself relaxing more with each step.

I was spellbound to see the crystal-clear water and bright sun. It was like stepping into a postcard. I nudged Ali and asked while pointing at the neighboring island, "Is that the capital city of Malé?"

Ali nodded, "Yep, that's Malé. The boat's on its way from there to pick you up."

I was bubbling with excitement about all the new things I was about to experience, but deep down, I wished my mom, dad, and Ajju & Reena could have been there to see this beauty. It was mesmerizing.

A small white boat with "Taj Coral Reef" written on it arrived, and I eagerly stepped aboard. I found a cozy seat, took out my white headphones, and turned on my music. The gentle rhythms enhanced the boat ride as I watched the sky and the horizon of the silky-smooth sea. The boat rocked gently at its pace, and I soon fell asleep, waking up just a minute before reaching the resort where I was hired to work.

Upon my arrival, I met a pretty-looking Chinese intern whose name I swear I forgot before she even finished saying it. She had a bright smile and an infectious laugh, and I made a mental note to ask her name again later if only my memory was better! Then there was Shipra, a beautiful North Indian lady with an elegance that could make a Bollywood actress jealous. She greeted me warmly and instantly made me feel at ease with her friendly nature.

"Aago, bai kashe asa?" (Oh dear how are you?) These words seemed familiar. My ears stood up straight to someone's glee in my language Konkani. It was Praveen, I thought he drank two cups of coffee and a Red Bull before breakfast, especially when he found out I was from Goa, too! Praveen was known as a good Samaritan to all the Goans working in the Maldives. Praveen grinned and extended his hand. "Welcome to paradise! Hope you packed your sunscreen." I was excited to see what was in the store for me.

As I was introduced to the islanders, I also met a few more friends, Rachel & Rebecca, who worked in 'The JIVA Spa'.

The place reminded me of a military base in a remote part of India. Being a former NCC cadet, I was used to staying in setups like that, with their colonial style, drifted doors, and ancient-looking locks.

While I was excited to meet new people and explore new places, a part of me was sad to leave behind my loved ones, especially leaving Goa. I was accommodated in a decent six-sharing room, and some of my roommates assumed they would be my colleagues.

Feeling lonely and homesick, I kept telling my heart, "Just one month and you can run away from here." It made me feel better, even though I knew how easily we can fool our hearts. "Isn't it funny how we do that?" *Sid nodded in agreement.*

"After settling down and meeting new people, I faced the most difficult moment of the day, nighttime. Being the reigning champion of insomnia back then, I often found myself caught in a mental wrestling match between my mind and heart. It felt like being a ringmaster without any power to call the shots. When nothing else helped, my eyes took over, leaving my pillows soaked with tears by morning. Unintentionally, the famous Bollywood song kept ringing in my head, "*tujhe yaad na meri aayi*", (you did not remember me) nothing but to add to my emotional flood."

'Sid asked Shifora, "Why did you cry?" with a tinge of smirk on his face.

Shifora, noticing the smirk on Sid's face, replied with a grin, "Oh, you know, just giving my pillows their nightly bath. They were starting to feel left out."

Sid sniggered, and soon they were both laughing, the tension of the moment melting away in their shared humor.'

Eleven

Merging myself with the land

"Shifora, I'm curious, what was the moment you realized that moving to the island wasn't just an adventure but a major turning point in your life?" Sid Curious to know more.

Shifora's eyes softened, and she let out a thoughtful sigh.

"As the days went by, I threw myself into learning the ins and outs of the workplace. Surprisingly, I realized this was exactly what I had been looking for. I enjoyed the job immensely. My role was to look after the guests at our resort, which included welcoming them, completing their check-in formalities, giving property tours, and villa briefings, and providing information on the resort's facilities, excursions, and activities."

"Talking to the guests became my favorite part of the job. Each arrival brought a fresh opportunity to learn about different nationalities and cultures. I loved sharing stories about the Maldives, India, and Goa. It was like a cultural exchange program right there at the resort.

Once, a group of excited Italian tourists arrived. They were bursting with questions, like, 'What's the best local dish?' and 'Where can we find the most amazing snorkeling spots?' I told them about our delicious Maldivian cuisine, especially the mouthwatering fish dishes like Garudhiya, a fragrant fish soup, and Mas Huni, a traditional breakfast dish made with tuna, coconut, and onions. When it came to snorkeling, I pointed them to some hidden gems that only locals know about, like the vibrant reefs around Fotteyo Falhu and the crystal-clear waters of Banana Reef!"

Shifora
Working at a Maldiives Front Office

Similarly, a Japanese family was fascinated by the history of the Maldives, and I enjoyed explaining the islands' rich cultural heritage.

"Ah, I see you're interested in the history of the Maldives. Did you know these islands have a rich folklore and tradition dating back centuries?" I asked, spotting their interest.

"Oh? That sounds fascinating! Please tell us more," one of them responded, eyes and mouth wide open.

"Well, one of the popular folklore stories here is about a mystical creature called "Nakaiy," believed to protect the islands and its people. It's said that Nakaiy would appear during storms to guide fishermen to safety, and its sightings were considered good omens for a plentiful catch."

"That's incredible! Such a beautiful legend. Is there any special tradition associated with the islands?" the same guest interrupted.

"Absolutely! One of the unique traditions here is the "Bodu-Beru" dance and music. It's a rhythmic performance where dancers move to the beat of traditional drums. The dance is often accompanied by chanting and clapping, creating an energetic atmosphere that's quite mesmerizing." I explained.

"Wow, we'd love to witness that! Thank you for sharing these stories and traditions with us, Shifora." another lady from the group said with a sparkle in her eyes.

I loved those moments. It was like being a cultural ambassador for the Maldives, sharing our beautiful traditions and the amazing things this country has to offer.

Every day brought something new and exciting. The variety kept me on my toes, and the interactions made me forget about the homesickness that plagued my nights. As much as I missed my family and Goa, the job constantly reminded me why I had made this leap. It wasn't just about a career, it was about growth, adventure, and the thrill of the unknown.

"Oh! So you blended into the new place like a chameleon, huh?" Sid quipped.

"Not quite, there was still a twist in the tale," Shifora remarked, a hint of mystery in her voice.

Twelve

MD's Award Winner

"You mean a plot twist? Spill the beans!" Sid raised his eyebrows, leaning in intuitively. "And how did you end up anchoring yourself on an island?"

"Picture this," Shifora began with a smile. "You're trudging through your daily grind when, out of the blue, your manager summons you. How would you feel?"

"Depends. Am I getting a promotion or getting the boot?" Sid smirked. "Go on, don't keep me in suspense!"

Shifora shrieked. "Well, it's a bit of both, in a way. That day remains etched in my memory with the clarity of a vivid dream. When I got the call from Ela Fernandes, my Reporting Manager, it felt like the universe was conspiring to throw me into an epic new chapter. She summoned me to her office with that cryptic, knowing look on her face, one that seemed to promise both intrigue and a hint of something momentous.

"Shifora, come in," she said, her voice carrying a hint of

excitement. 'I have something to show you.' She waved a piece of paper like a magician revealing their final trick.

My interest was on high alert, mixed with a swirl of apprehension. My heart pounded like a drum, and my stomach did somersaults. Was this the moment I'd been dreading? A complaint? A mistake? My mind was racing through a million scenarios, each more dramatic than the last.

Ela handed me the paper, and as I scanned it, my eyes went wide. There, in bold, glowing praise were Anurag's kind words about my hospitality. He had mentioned my name!

'He mentioned my name,' I whispered, barely able to believe it.

'Yes,' Ela confirmed, her smile stretching as if it could light up the entire office. 'And this is only within two weeks of you joining us. You're already a star.'

A ripple of applause erupted from my colleagues who had gathered at the door. The sound of clapping and cheers washed over me like a tidal wave of pride and joy. It was recognition I hadn't dared to dream of so soon, a validation of everything I had hoped for.

At that moment, I felt a surge of elation, this was the dopamine hit I needed, the affirmation that all my efforts were paying off. I grinned from ear to ear, feeling as if I were on top of the world.

"Ela continued, her voice full of enthusiasm. 'This feedback will be added to our 'STARS' system here at TAJ. Every time a guest mentions a staff member's name, that staff member earns 10 points. To reach the MD's Club, the highest level, you need over 1000 points."

I was captivated, my eyes wide with wonder. 'A thousand points? That sounds like a lot.'

'It is,' Ela agreed, her tone confident. 'But I have a feeling you'll make it. Keep up the great work.'

"That moment changed everything for me. No more tears at night, no more daydreams of returning to Goa in a month. Instead, I dove into my work with renewed vigor, driven by the challenge and the desire to excel in hospitality. By 2014, I had done it, I broke records and achieved a historical milestone at Taj Coral by winning the MD's Club. And that wasn't the end. I clinched the trophy again in 2015 and 2016."

"The 'STARS' system wasn't just a recognition program; it became my driving force, of excellence. Every guest interaction was a chance to make a mark, to leave a positive impression, and to earn those coveted points. It wasn't just about the accolades; it was about becoming the best version of myself, one interaction at a time."

Thirteen

Talwar of Marriage

"Two years had passed, and I had comfortably settled into my job. Life was smooth, like a perfectly brewed cup of chai. But as any Indian girl knows, the "talwar" (sword) of marriage always hung over our heads. And for me, it was no different. Proposals came in from various corners of India, and my mother was on a relentless mission to get me married. I dodged it like Neo in The Matrix. She had a singular vision for me, a nice Christian wedding, a decent boy by my side, and, preferably, my degree hung somewhere I'd never actually need it. To her, my education was always secondary, something to keep me 'occupied' until a suitable guy came along.

She would say, "Who's going to marry a girl with these many books on her head?" According to her, studying too much meant I'd be a "difficult" girl, a girl that no good Christian boy would dare try to 'control.' Independence, as she liked to remind me, was 'for people who can't get a husband.'

And the boys she did find! She'd introduce me to the most 'eligible' bachelors, the ones whose only qualification seemed to be that they were, well, 'Christian and breathing.' Her standards for them were minimal but for me?, The bar was sky-high. "A respectable man doesn't want a wife with her head in books," she'd say, wagging a finger as if I'd somehow committed a crime against our entire lineage.

She had a whole list of reasons why I needed to slow down, stop studying so hard, and start thinking about my 'future'which, to her, was synonymous with marriage and motherhood. Independence? to her, that was just another word for 'loneliness.' Her perfect world for me was one where I'd have a husband to lean on financially and emotionally and books that didn't have too many pages for me to get lost in."

And while I'm grateful for her care, I couldn't help but wish, sometimes, that she'd understand I could have both a career and a life. But to her, that just sounds exhausting.

So here we are, years later, with her still on the lookout and me still quietly dodging every not-so-qualified bachelor she waves in my direction. If my career and independence don't count as achievements, I suppose I'll have to wait and see if her matchmaking skills improve… but I'm not holding my breath!

One evening as I was wrapping up my work, I received a call from my mother. I answered with a sigh, already anticipating the topic.

"Baaie, how are you?". she asked with the most suspicious tone.

"Good Mom", I answered bracing myself.

"Nothing much, Just you know, I had a chat with Mrs. D'costa today," she said casually.

"Oh, the same one who stays near the road to the church? I remember her son had 3 cats." I replied to keep it light.

"Yes, yes," she guffawed, "but wasn't I talking about her son, though? Speaking of sons, I remember Maria Aunty had called up regarding a prospecting match for you from Pune. He worked as a software engineer in a well-known company and was well-settled. Above all, he was from a very good family." she finally blurted out, unable to contain her excitement.

"Mom, I am not ready". Trying to keep my tone steady. "I am doing well here, "Mom, What's the rush?"

"What's the rush? Are you getting any younger day by day?" she disputed.

"But I am just 26. I promise that by 29, I will feel ready for marriage." I kept my fingers crossed and I knew that I was hoping against hope. I counter-replied.

"Ready by 29? Then by what time we will get you married? 31? Do you think there is a showroom for grooms? There is a thing called 'search', which takes almost a year and a half." Mom emphasized SEARCH as if that was the much-needed oxygen of her life.

"Arrggh. Ok, mom. You win." I gave in, knowing that when moms prepare the question paper, you don't get to skip any questions. She makes sure that you get to attempt everything without any options.

"Finally, I got sucked into my daily grind at work. But every time I called home, it was nothing but marriage talks. Dodging those calls was like dodging bullets in a Bollywood movie. Everyone around me was busy finding their "happily ever after," and here I was, still getting butterflies from SRK's romantic movies, those "sarvagun sampann" husbands from Ekta Kapoor TV shows, and Taylor Swift's fantasy world."

"Life seemed to be on autopilot, just cruising along. I didn't have any grand plans back then, just taking care of my parents and trying to keep my skills and hobbies from gathering too much dust. But they were neglected, poor things.

"I read somewhere that when everything feels calm, it's a sign that a storm is brewing. Little did I know, that storm was about to hit me like a rogue wave. The kind that knocks you off your feet and changes everything. The storm swept me away and I never returned to my old self again."

Fourteen

Finding companion

"Being from Goa, how did you survive on the island? Did you even have friends there? What did you do during your free time?" Sid's unfeigned interest widened.

"Of Course, I had friends." Shifora continued. "Praveen, Shipra, Rachel, and Rebecca were some of them who were very close to me.

"We shared moments of joy and sorrow, often going on fishing trips in the deep sea or enjoying beach bonfires under the stars. We went snorkeling, Swimming and sometimes went shopping on the mainland - Malé. We always ensured to support each other, and that's how we built a strong bond. Over time, they all moved out of the islands for their own plans. Praveen got transferred to Goa. Shipra went back to Delhi and got married to the love of her life. Rachel went to Mumbai to support her family, and Rebecca and I were the last ones remaining. I could feel the emptiness when all the others had left, especially when Rachel went. I felt homesick and lonely once more, reminiscent of my initial days on the island.

"I don't see Arif anywhere though?" Sid Interrupted

"At that time Arif was just a colleague, I knew him just as another employee like us. Shifora advocated.

"I see, just colleagues uhh?" Sarcasm poured out from Sid's face.

Shifora nodded with a sip of the tea in her mouth. And then continued, "While I was going through this grief of parting with friends, I noticed one of my colleagues, Arif, sitting outside a staff tuck shop. The usually happy and vibrant person seemed a little down that day. Arif was a tall, dark, and well-groomed guy, with a chubby physique that added to his jovial appearance. He had a warm smile that instantly put people at ease, and his easy-going nature made him popular among guests and colleagues. Arif was from Maldives and had a very good reputation for his work and behavior among all nationalities in the resort".

"While reminiscing, one incident with Arif stood out vividly in my memory. It was during our early days working together at the resort, when Arif had messaged me out of the blue, suggesting we should be best friends. I remember reading his message and laughing it off, replying with a casual, "Come on, Arif, we're just colleagues!" Little did I know back then that he would eventually become my closest companion on the island."

Sid, shaking his head. "Sounds like something straight out of a rom-com. Did you ever imagine back then that you two would become so close?"

Shifora with a hint of nostalgia in her eyes. "Honestly, no. At that time, I thought he was just being his usual quirky self. But as days turned into months, and we faced the challenges of island life together, we naturally grew closer. It was like the universe had other plans for us.

Arif, being the easygoing person he is, took it in stride but didn't give up. He would tease me now and then about my initial rejection of his friendship offer, making light-hearted jokes about how he was hurt by my rejection. I, of course, would playfully roll my eyes and remind him that we were still just colleagues.

That usually vibrant and cheerful Arif appeared unusually down that day. He sat outside the staff tuck shop, a cigarette hidden in his hand as he pretended not to smoke. I approached him, concern etched on my face.

"Arif, is everything okay with you?" I asked softly, noting his troubled expression.

Arif looked up, trying to muster a smile but failing to conceal the distress in his eyes. "Not really," he replied, his voice tinged with frustration. "I'm not sure how much longer I can keep this up."

I prodded gently, "um keep up what?" I was measuring each word so nothing would stab him even unintentionally.

He took a deep breath, his shoulders slumping. "Remember that group of guests in-house? They've complained to us, and everyone's pointing fingers at my department. With the Head of the department away, they're blaming me. It's clear that we're not at fault, the guest is."

I could feel Arif's frustration and humility as he spoke. It wasn't uncommon in the hospitality industry for blame to be misplaced, yet it was disheartening every time. Arif was known for his dedication and integrity among colleagues of all nationalities in the resort. To see him under such pressure was unsettling.

"I'm sorry to hear that, Arif," I said sincerely. "It must be tough handling all of this alone."

Arif nodded, his brow furrowed. "I just don't know how to prove our innocence. It's affecting the team's morale and my confidence in handling situations like this."

I placed a reassuring hand on his shoulder. "I understand. It's not easy, but remember, everyone here knows your worth. You've always handled these situations with grace and competence."

He managed a weak smile. "Thanks, Shifora. I needed to hear that."

Sid leaned back in his chair, smirking. "Ah, so the great Arif has a weak spot after all. Here I thought he was invincible, like some kind of hospitality superhero."

Shifora shot him a playful glare, shaking her head. "Oh, come on, Sid. Even superheroes have their moments of doubt. It's what makes them human." She paused, her expression softening. "And it's what makes them stronger in the end."

Sid Rolled his eyes,

Shifora Continued "As we talked, I realized how much pressure Arif was under and how deeply it was affecting him. It was a stark reminder of the challenges faced in the service industry, where maintaining a smile and positivity often masked the struggles underneath."

"However, as time went on, we started spending more time together outside of work. We would go for walks on the beach after our shifts, and grab meals together, and eventually, we both realized that our bond had grown much deeper than just colleagues. It became a running joke between us that Arif was still waiting for my acceptance into the "best friend" club.

You know, when friends start crossing into new territory, things are bound to get interesting. What happens when the line between "just friends" and "something more" starts to blur?"

Sid leaned back with a smirk, his eyes twinkling with fascination. "Ah, the classic dilemma of friendships on the edge of something more. It's like watching a thriller where you're on the edge of your seat, just waiting for the next twist. I can't help but wonder: when that line starts to blur, what kind of fireworks are we in for? Sounds like the kind of plot that makes you forget to blink."

Fifteen

Love in an Islander

'Sid leaned in, a smirk on his face. "You know, Shifora, I'm dying to hear more about you and Arif. What was the most ridiculous thing you two did on that island?"

Shifora chuckled, "Oh, Sid, where do I even begin? We were always finding ways to entertain ourselves."

Sid raised an eyebrow. "Like what? Did you two ever pull off some grand scheme?"

Shifora grinned. "There was this one time Arif decided to prank the whole staff by pretending we had a celebrity guest. Everyone was running around, trying to get a glimpse of this imaginary star."

Sid chortled. "That's classic! But come on, there's got to be more."

Shifora leaned back, a thoughtful look in her eyes. "Well, there was another time we tried to create our version of a reality show. We called it 'Island Survivor' and challenged each other to live off the land for a day. Let's just say Arif wasn't thrilled about eating coconuts and fish all day."

Sid shook his head, still smiling. "You two were quite the dynamic duo. But seriously, it sounds like you had a pretty special bond."

Shifora's expression softened, her voice drifting into nostalgia. "Yeah, we looked out for each other. We weren't just colleagues anymore. By then, we'd spent three years at TAJ Coral, and after work, we'd end up chatting late into the night about everything movies, religion, you name it. We'd even debate how Islam and Christianity were related. Arif usually won our trivia games on the phone, he had a weird talent for that! , and he was always painting in his free time, blasting David Guetta in the background, totally in his element."

"Oh, and his PS3! Back then, everyone in the Maldives seemed obsessed with getting one, and Arif was no exception. It was such a simple life. Just a few things, a few friends, and a whole lot of heart."

"I remember the time when I surprised Arif on his birthday. He had never celebrated his birthdays before, so I decided to change that. I secretly decorated his room and ordered a cake. When he walked in and saw everything, he was overwhelmed. "Oh Shifora, I like the way you always made me feel special," Arif said, hiding his tears under his smile. I knew it was a common gesture where I'm from, but it was something entirely new to him, and it made him incredibly happy. Similarly, there were times when Arif surprised me too, like the time he arranged a private dinner on the beach under the stars. Those moments were precious to us, little sparks of joy in our simple island life."

"Sounds like you were quite the birthday fairy, Shifora," Sid teased, a playful spark in his eye. "Did you have a stash of confetti and balloons ready for any occasion?"

Shifora rolled her eyes, and said Satirically, "Oh. I carried a party kit in my back pocket at all times. You never know when you need to turn someone's day around."

Sid with jelaous grin, "I bet Arif was secretly waiting for his next surprise after that. You set a pretty high bar, you know."

Shifora's eyes reflecting a mix of nostalgia and amusement. "Maybe I did. But it was worth it to see him so happy. Those little moments what kept us going on that tiny island."

"I fondly remember how Arif used to call the front office every day at 6 pm to get some guest information. It was only later that he revealed he used to call just to chat, even though he already had the information."

Sid said softly, breaking the spell of Shifora's reminiscence. "Wow, he called just to hear your voice? Arif had it bad, huh?"

It was impossible for to Shifora laugh. "Well, what can I say? I guess my voice was just that soothing."

Sid teased, "So, Arif won you over with his trivia skills and PS3 prowess, huh? I need to step up my game."

Shifora playfully responded, "Oh, Sid, you had your charm. Arif and I just had a lot in common in terms of understanding, you know?"

Joyous Sid "I know, I know. But seriously, it sounds like you guys had a great connection."

Shifora nodded. "Yeah, we did. It was like we understood even the silence between us."

Sid mimic to smile, but his eyes betrayed a hint of jealousy. Shifora caught it immediately, the way his gaze shifted and lingered a moment too long.

She raised an eyebrow, a teasing smile playing on her lips.

"Oh? Jealous much, Sid?"

Sid flustered, pulled at his ears dramatically, trying to play it off. "I'm all ears about what happened next," he insisted, looking somewhat ridiculous as he tugged on his earlobes.

Shifora broke up with the laughter, unable to hold back. "You look ridiculous," she said, nudging him lightly, but there was a warmth in her eyes. Somewhere beneath his act, she sensed the care he was trying to mask.

"In a resort setup like that, where we could hardly step out of the island on our weekly offs due to various reasons like bad weather, inconvenient boat timings, or being broke by the end of the month. There were times when we planned a trip to the city, only to get stranded for days due to the boat breaking down in the middle of the sea. For instance, Rachel once went to the city to complete her bank formalities, but the weather suddenly turned, and she had to stay there for two days because no boats were allowed to ply.'

"Another time, we all went to a team-building activity on another island, and while returning, the boat's engine failed, leaving us stranded in the middle of the sea for hours. We had shifts the next morning, so it was a horrible experience staying on the boat. With not much to do, yes, we could swim or hit the gym, but we were confined to those limited activities and interactions. Eventually, we started feeling that this was all there was to the world. All those people around us were everything. Nothing beyond that. Like one of my friends rightly said, "tum hi mere Shahrukh Khan, and tum hi mere Salman Khan" (you were my Shahrukh Khan, you were my Salman Khan). That's it."

Sixteen

He is the one

"Over a period, I somehow molded myself with Arif and slowly realized that I started liking everything about him. The way he took care of me, stood by me, thought of me, appreciated me, respected me, cared for me, made me feel special, motivated me, and supported me to the extent that I felt safe around him. He even reminded me of my father in many of his habits, especially when we discussed politics. Just like my dad, who supported every decision I made in my life, Arif did too. Of course, I was PAPA ki PARI (daddy's angel), and those feelings were countless. Everything seemed picture-perfect. I found myself daydreaming about a future with him."

Sid leaned with a wicked sparkle in his eye. "So who was on their knees first? I am sure, Arif?"

Shifora tittered, "Oh, you think so? Neither of us. It was more like we slowly fell into place together. No grand proposals or dramatic moments, just a gradual realization."

Sid raised an eyebrow. "No way? I pictured him with a ring and all."

"Nope, just two people finding their way to each other." She answered.

"As I mentioned, we used to talk a lot. We discussed every topic in detail, weighing the pros and cons. For weeks, I hesitated, unsure if I should reveal my feelings. What if it ruined our friendship? What if he didn't feel the same way? My heart was a whirlwind of doubts and fears. He was from a different faith, a different country, a different culture, with a different upbringing, we had so many differences between us and countless reasons not to unite."

But then, inspired by a line from my favorite book, Pride and Prejudice, which said, "Take the risk or lose the chance," I decided to muster the courage to share my feelings with him.

"I could see a mix of surprise and joy on his face. His eyes widened for a moment, and then he broke into a soft, heartfelt smile. There was a light in his eyes that hadn't been there before, a kind of relief and happiness. "Shifora," he said, his voice almost a whisper, "I've been wanting to say this for so long, but I didn't know how. I feel the same way." He reached out and gently took my hand, his touch warm and reassuring. "I can't believe we were both feeling this and didn't know it. But now, we do."

That's when we had that quintessential rom-com moment, "Is this love? Do we love each other?" From that day, we started seeing each other as more than just colleagues and friends. And yes, we accepted it. We were happy and shared this news with everyone on the island and our families."

"Any guesses on reactions?" Shifora questioned.

Sid rolled his eyes dramatically. I am on my toes now."

Seventeen

Romance under the stars

While I was in a relationship with Arif, I felt an incredible sense of joy knowing I had someone of my own to call, talk to, and share my thoughts with. Of course, there were plenty of people eager to point out the obvious differences between us, our cultures, religions, languages, and the small matter of being from different countries. But I was determined. I believed we could make it work and live our own happily ever after. I mean, if Heer Ranjha and Romeo and Juliet could almost pull it off without WhatsApp, why couldn't we?

We spent countless nights under the stars, discussing our future and dreaming about the life we'd have together. Those conversations were filled with excitement and hope, punctuated by laughter and occasional bouts of seriousness. Oh, I cannot forget those newly launched songs of Sam Smith and Ed Sheeran, I don't remember how many times we have replaced them. as if we had only these couple of songs in our playlist.

"Thinking out loud?", Sid Enchanted,

"Yes," Shifora continued, "Perfect" and "I am not the only one- by Sam Smith."

"Wow!! romantic uhh? Sid giggled.

———————-

"I can't believe we're planning a life together," Arif often said, his eyes twinkling with joy. "It feels surreal, like a dream I don't want to wake up from."

"I know, right?" I replied, feeling a mix of excitement and nervousness. "But tell me, Arif, how do you picture our future home?"

Arif leaned back, looking thoughtful. "I imagine it cozy, with lots of natural light and a garden in the back where we can grow our vegetables. And a little reading nook for you filled with all your favorite books."

"Don't forget the kitchen," I added with a grin. "I need a big kitchen where I can try out all those recipes I've been downloading."

Arif snikered. "As long as I get to be your official, culinary confidant, I'm all for it."

One night, lying on a blanket under the stars, Arif suddenly asked, "If we could travel anywhere together, where would you want to go first?"

I thought for a moment, then said, "I've always wanted to take you to Goa. It's my hometown, and there's something magical about it. It's not just the beaches, it's the vibe, the relaxed culture, the open-mindedness. There are festivals all year round, the mountains, the villages, the traditions and rituals. Goa is a place where unity thrives among neighbors, a truly secular place."

Arif charmed, "Perfect. We'll make it our honeymoon destination. Just you, me, and the vibrant, welcoming spirit of Goa."

We often talked about our wedding plans, too. "Do you think we'll manage to blend both our traditions?" I asked one evening, feeling a bit apprehensive.

"Absolutely," Arif said confidently. "We can have a ceremony that respects both our faiths. A celebration that brings our families together. I want it to be a day where we honor our backgrounds and create something uniquely ours."

The thought of it made me emotional. "I've always imagined walking down the aisle with my mom by my side, and you waiting for me at the end, looking nervous but happy."

"I'll probably be more nervous than happy," Arif joked, but I knew he was looking forward to it just as much as I was. "And I can already see Palomi in the front row, tearing up and clapping the loudest."

Palomi was our rock, our cheerleader. While everyone else was skeptical and raising eyebrows, Palomi had unwavering faith in us. "So, when's the big day?" she constantly asked, her excitement contagious.

"One particularly memorable night, we were caught in a sudden downpour. Instead of rushing inside, Arif pulled me into his arms, and we danced in the rain," Shifora recalled, her eyes lighting up with the memory.

"Here's to the future Mrs. Arif," he said, spinning me around as we both laughed like kids.

Sid interrupted, his tone laced with surprise, "But I remember you never liked the rain." Shifora pleased, pleasantly surprised that Sid remembered such a small detail after all these years.

"When you're in love, it changes you upside down, you start liking things you never thought you would," Shifora clarified.

Sid tried to smile, though it didn't quite reach his eyes. "What? Then that's not love. That's just losing yourself in the moment."

Shifora continued, ignoring the slight jab. "You know, I teased Arif, saying that dancing in the rain wasn't exactly what I had in mind for a romantic night."

"But it's memorable, right?" Arif had countered, his grin infectious. "And besides, you look beautiful with your hair all wet."

"Flattery will get you everywhere," Shifora added with a soft laugh. "But honestly, we spent so many evenings like that, planning our future, talking about starting a family, and dreaming about our life together."

Sid leaned back, his expression shifting as he broke the flow of her narrative. "Well, that's what romance is all about, right? The flow. But I've got to say, Shifora, you plan a lot for someone who claims to be swept up by love."

Shifora paused, feeling the undercurrent of Sid's words. "Maybe I did plan a lot, but it felt right at the time. We even binge-watched wedding videos until I saw flower arrangements in my sleep. We designed and ordered my wedding dress months in advance."

Sid tilted his head, a hint of sarcasm creeping into his voice. "Ah, so let me guess, you had a checklist for romance too? Anything else Arif had to tick off the list?"

Shifora's smile faltered, and she looked down for a moment. "Yeah, I guess we did. But that's what made it feel real, you know?"

It's funny how everyone saves up for their wedding, right? And when I say "save," I mean mentally, financially, emotionally, and yes, physically too. Weddings are the ultimate culmination of all your efforts, or at least, that's what I thought. And let's be real, it's the one day you can justify spending a small fortune on a dress you'll wear once.

While this thought of 'saving' ruled my mind, I knew I had to 'save up mentally' for another challenge. Guess what?"

Eighteen

Unfolding the Wedding Blind

"Oh, that's the most awaited one: convincing your families!" Sid beamed with his neck held high as if he was the only one in the class who knew the answer.

"Ah, well, that's an interesting story." Shifora acknowldeged.

"How was Arif's reaction to your wedding plan?" Sid interrupted Shifora with his hiked-up Curiosity.

"Well, I was on cloud nine those days," Shifora began, a wistful smile on her face. But when I mentioned the grand celebration plans to Arif, he seemed indifferent."

"Why don't we have grand celebrations?" I questioned him.

Arif sat back, his brow furrowing in contemplation. "Why can't we just sign the documents and finish it off?"

My heart sank a little at his words. "Arif," I protested gently, "our wedding is more than just signing papers. It's about celebrating our love, our families coming together, and embracing our traditions."

He sighed, running a hand through his hair. "I understand, but all that pomp and grandeur… it's not necessary."

"But Arif," I insisted, trying to keep my disappointment at bay, "This is Goa. Our weddings are known for joyous celebrations, vibrant colors, and rich traditions. I want our wedding to be memorable, filled with music, dance, and laughter."

Arif looked conflicted, torn between my enthusiasm and his reservations. "I don't want to disappoint you, Shifora," he said softly. "But I've never been one for big celebrations. Can't we keep it simple?"

I felt a pang of frustration mingled with understanding. "I want us to start our life together with a celebration that we'll cherish forever," I explained earnestly. "It's not just about us; it's about sharing our happiness with everyone we love."

Arif hesitated, then spoke quietly, "I don't want anyone from my workplace to know that I am Marrying somebody from another faith. People can get jealous and give us the evil eye."

"But, Arif, they all know we are in a relationship." I proclaimed.

"Being in a relationship is okay but Marrying is different." Arif Interrupted

I was taken aback. "But Arif, our wedding should be a time of joy and sharing with those who care about us."

Arif nodded, looking uncomfortable. "I understand your point, but I feel it's safer this way, let's keep it quiet and intimate."

She knew what mattered most was the love they shared and the presence of those closest to them. And in that moment, she was certain it would be perfect, so she gave a agreeing smile.

As Shifora recounted the conversation to Sid, she couldn't help but laugh softly. "You know, Sid, it wasn't easy. Arif and I had very different ideas about our wedding day."

Sid curious, leaning forward with interest. "Sounds like there were some spirited discussions."

"Oh, you have no idea," Shifora replied, recalling the animated debates they had. "At times, it felt like we were speaking different languages. I wanted the festivity of Goa, and he wanted simplicity."

"And how did you find common ground?" Sid asked, intrigued by their journey.

"We compromised," Shifora explained with a shrug. "We found a balance that honored both of our wishes. In the end, what mattered most was that we were together, starting our journey as husband and wife."

Shifora paused, a fond smile playing on her lips. "It taught us the importance of understanding and respecting each other's perspectives, Sid. Our wedding may not have been the grand celebration I initially dreamed of, but it was beautiful in its way."

Sid nodded thoughtfully. "Sometimes, the most meaningful celebrations are the ones where love and compromise shine through."

"And that's exactly what our wedding day was," Shifora concluded with a smile.

Nineteen

Love and Job Juggling

"Why was that after the blissful honeymoon phase, everything seemed to unravel so quickly? Was it just me, or did everyone else feel the weight of expectation and suspicion too?" Shifora's mind raced as she reflected on the sudden shift in her work environment.

Sid, noticing Shifora's pensive look, leaned in with a teasing grin. "Lost in thought, huh? Or are you just plotting how to get the office to stop treating you like a villain in a soap opera?"

"Was I thinking that loud?" She paused, a thoughtful look crossing her face. "I just realized something about the work environment those days…"

"Go on," Sid encouraged, sensing there was more to her Disclosure.

"The reality began to creep in, and not the romantic reality we were planning in Goa. Suddenly, at work, I became the prime suspect for every minor mishap, as if someone had decided I was the office's official scapegoat. Colleagues who were once my cheerleaders now eyed me with suspicion. Arif faced similar issues in his department. Every morning, he was picked apart in meetings and accused of using his position for personal gain."

"Seriously, you'd think he was smuggling resort towels home or something! The allegations were absurd. We never misused our positions or indulged in personal matters during duty hours. Yet, the pressure mounted on both sides, making it increasingly difficult to stay at the resort. So, we found ourselves at a crossroads. It was more like a complex roundabout with two exits. First, I had to choose between my job and the person I loved. No contest, I chose Arif. Second, either he had to leave his job, or I did."

"And guess what? I volunteered as a tribute. Besides, with our grand wedding plans in Goa, I needed some time off anyway. So, taking a leap of faith, I decided to quit. It seemed like the right decision at the time, considering the ever-thickening plot around us."

Sid, who had been listening intently, finally spoke up. "You actually quit your job? That's a huge step, But why suddenly they shifted their gears against you?""

Shifora nodded, feeling a mix of nostalgia and conviction. "Yeah, it was. But it felt right at the time. I believed in our plan."

Sid raised an eyebrow. "Wow. That's some serious commitment. I'm not sure I could have done that."

Shifora justifying, "Well, when you're in love, you sometimes do crazy things. Besides, I was excited about the future we were planning."

Sid leaned back, still processing. "I get it. It's just… a lot. I hope it all worked out the way you envisioned."

Shifora blithe softly, remembering those days of hope and excitement. "We had our dreams, and we were determined to make them happen. But, as you'll see, life had a few surprises in store for us."

"Before handing in my resignation, Arif and I sat down for one final, serious planning session. Our blueprint for happiness was meticulous, complete with color-coded post-its and perhaps a touch of overconfidence. The plan was simple. I'd quit my job, we'd get married in Goa in three months, and then Arif would work his magic to find me a new job back in the Maldives."

"Okay, so you'll be job-hunting while I'm bridal shopping," I said, trying to keep my voice steady.

Arif grinned. "Absolutely. And don't worry, I'll find something great for you in Malé."

"After the wedding, we'd live in Malé City for better job prospects, hopefully on a dependent visa. Arif would also look for a better job, and we both planned to study further, have a family, and in ten years, move to Goa permanently. Yes, Arif promised we'd settle in Goa eventually. It was the life we envisioned together."

Twenty

Truly Blind for you

"One day, amidst the hustle and bustle of my daily work, Mrs. Malik, a colleague with a penchant for drama, sashayed over with a twinkle in her eye and all the subtlety of a seasoned gossipmonger.

"My dear," she began, leaning in conspiratorially, "This relationship of yours? Not the wisest choice, if you ask me. You're far too sorted and ambitious to end up in the doldrums with someone like him."

I couldn't resist but chuckle at Mrs. Malik's forthrightness, but her words struck a chord nonetheless. She painted a rather bleak picture of Arif's supposed shortcomings. "No grand family estate, no home to call his own, and the occasional empty pantry," she listed as if ticking off items on a grocery list.

Before she could say anything further, I interrupted with a smile. "Mrs. Malik, I'm committed to Arif, flaws and all. I'll stand by him and his family through thick and thin."

That evening, with Mrs. Malik's words still ringing in my ears, I confronted Arif about the rumors. To my relief, he met my concerns with reassurance. With a charming smile and a twinkle in his eye, he vowed to address any challenges that lay ahead.

"Don't worry," he said confidently. "I'll take care of everything. My family, your family, you, everyone will be fine. I promise."

His words were like a soothing balm. Not only was I impressed, but I also felt proud to have a man like Arif standing by me so strongly. After all, he said he would take care of the family, right? And that's always been my weakness.

Sid, who was listening intently, smirked. "So, Mrs. Malik thought you were too ambitious, huh? Sounds like she didn't know what she was talking about."

"Yeah, Sid, she underestimated both of us. Arif and I were a team, and we knew we could handle whatever came our way" Shifora expressed softly.

Sid leaned back, still processing. "I guess love does make you do crazy things. But hey, if it works, it works."

Shifora exhaled, thinking back to those days of determination and hope. "Exactly, Sid. We were ready to face the world together, come what may."

Twenty-One

The Revelation

"Those days, my mind was entirely consumed by wedding plans with Arif, as if I was in a wedding planning hangover. Out of the blue one day, during dinner, I found myself saying, "You know, most people in the Maldives get married young?". Naturally, recalling Mrs. Maalik's words. "Mrs. Maalik was counting on her fingers, listing all the young brides and grooms she's known. She had a whole list ready!" I tried to mimic Mrs. Maalik's exaggerated gestures."

As I laughed, I noticed Arif's face grow darker with each word I spoke. The playful light in his eyes dimmed, and his smile faltered. He froze, like a statue, mid-motion, the fork slipping from his fingers and clattering onto the table. My laughter died in my throat, replaced by a tightening in my chest. "Hey, what's wrong?" I asked softly, leaning forward. His jaw clenched, and his breath hitched, his eyes locking onto mine, wide and startled, as if he'd seen something someone unseen. The air between us thickened, and for a moment, everything felt heavy, suspended in time, his lips parted as if to speak, then closed again, uncertain.

I reached across the table, my hand gently touching his. "Arif, talk to me," I urged, my heart pounding. The room felt smaller, the walls closing in as I waited for his response. The flickering candlelight cast shadows on his face, highlighting the conflict in his eyes. I could feel the tension building, a knot tightening in my chest.

He became unusually quiet, his eyes avoiding mine. I caught him fidgeting with the napkin, twisting it absentmindedly. "Arif?" I asked gently, but he just smiled, a little too quickly, brushing it off with a casual shrug.

As the day wore on, the unease between us grew. I'd catch him staring off into space, lost in thought, then shaking his head as if to clear it. His jaw would tighten whenever the conversation steered toward anything remotely serious, and when I'd laugh or try to lighten the mood, his responses felt distant, almost mechanical.

We spent the rest of the evening walking in silence, the weight of whatever he was holding back lingering like a shadow over us. Every time I thought he'd finally speak, his lips would part but then close again, and he'd change the subject, leaving me wondering what was going on inside his head.

Finally, he took a deep breath, his shoulders sagging as if a heavy burden weighed them down. "It's just…," he began, his voice barely above a whisper. "The idea of marriage brings up a lot of expectations and pressures. Especially in our community."

His words hung in the air, heavy and laden with unspoken

fears. I squeezed his hand, trying to offer reassurance. "We don't have to follow anyone else's expectations," I said softly. "It's our journey, our story. We can write it however we want."

Arif's eyes glistened with unshed tears, and for a moment, I saw the depth of his vulnerability. It broke my heart to see him struggling, to see the weight of tradition and expectation bearing down on him. But at that moment, I also felt a surge of determination. We would face this together, no matter what.

"I wanted to tell you," he confessed finally, his voice barely above a whisper. "But I was afraid. Afraid of losing you. I never meant to hide anything."

"As his words hung in the air, heavy with unspoken truths. I felt a knot tighten in my stomach, a sinking feeling spreading through me. "And?" I pressed, my voice betraying a hint of nervousness.

Arif hesitated, his gaze momentarily dropping to the floor before meeting mine once more. "There's more," he began, his tone somber. "I….. I …I have been married before."

Twenty-Two

The Acceptance

"His admission landed like a thunderclap, unexpected and jarring. I felt my heart skip a beat, my mind struggling to comprehend what he had just revealed. Married? How could this be?

He continued, his voice tinged with regret and sadness as he unraveled the story of his previous marriage. "We were young," he began, his gaze distant. "Full of dreams and plans for the future. But life has a way of testing you in ways you never expect."

Arif paused, his eyes reflecting a deep sorrow. "Our relationship was supposed to be built on love, but it quickly became clear that it was all about money. She lived in the city, while I was tied to my responsibilities at the resort. Every penny I earned, I sent to her, hoping to support our future together. But she spent it all, and kept requesting more and more."

His voice grew strained as he recounted the conflicts. "It

wasn't just the spending. We fought constantly. Whenever I couldn't send enough money, she'd lash out, accusing me of not caring, not loving her enough. I remember one night, after a particularly grueling day, she called me, furious that I hadn't sent her extra cash for a new dress she wanted. I tried to explain that we needed to save, but she wouldn't listen. 'Do you want me to look like a beggar?' she screamed."

Arif's hands trembled slightly, the memory still raw. "The arguments became a regular occurrence. She'd go out with her friends, spending the money I gave her for emergencies on lavish dinners and parties. The emotional connection we once had faded away, replaced by a bitter resentment. It felt like she was using me as her ATM, and no matter how hard I tried, it was never enough."

He sighed, the pain evident in his voice. "One night, after another heated argument over money, I realized I couldn't take it anymore. She was living a life of luxury in the city while I was working myself to the bone at the resort. The distance wasn't just physical; it was emotional and spiritual. I felt like a prisoner in a relationship that was supposed to be my sanctuary."

His eyes met mine, filled with raw emotion and anguish. "I gave up on the relationship because it was destroying me. The constant demands, the fights, the feeling of being used—it was too much. I told her it was over, and though it broke my heart, I knew it was the right decision."

Each word seemed to add weight to the shocking suspense, each detail painting a complex portrait of his past. His eyes met mine, and I saw the pain and vulnerability there, the scars left by a love that once was. The admission hung in the air, raw and unfiltered, rendering me speechless as I struggled to process the depth of his past.

"I didn't know how to tell you all of these," Arif admitted, his gaze pleading for understanding.

His words echoed in the silence that followed, leaving me grappling with a mix of emotions, disbelief, hurt, and a lingering sense of betrayal. I had thought I knew Arif and trusted him with my heart and my future. And yet, here I was, confronted with a truth that threatened to unravel everything.

"I… I don't know what to say," I finally managed, my voice barely above a whisper. "How could you keep this from me?"

The silence that followed felt like a chasm opening between us. My pulse quickened, and I took a deep breath, trying to steady myself for what might come next. The air felt thick, suffocating, weighed down by the gravity of Arif's confession about his previous marriage. Every second that passed seemed to stretch longer as if time itself hesitated in the face of this uncovering the story.

I looked into his eyes, desperate for answers, searching for any sign of hesitation or evasion. But all I found was the quiet torment etched into his face. My stomach churned, and a sinking feeling took root deep inside me.

"So, this is what you've been hiding," I whispered, the words tasting bitter on my tongue. I realized how much he had kept from me and how much we were still strangers in ways that mattered most. "What else don't I know?"

Arif shifted uncomfortably, his gaze dropping to the floor. He ran a hand through his hair, clearly grappling with the weight of his past. I could see the hesitation, the distance forming between us. A wall I hadn't known existed until now.

A knot formed in my throat, the kind you can't swallow down. "Was this… was this ever real for you?" I asked, my voice breaking as I dared to ask the question I wasn't sure I wanted answered. His silence was deafening, and the more he held back, the more my heart began to crack."

The weight of his silence was enough to make me wonder if this was the beginning of the end.

Twenty-Three

Stunned Silence

"I stood abruptly, the chair scraping loudly against the floor. "I need some air," I muttered, barely glancing at him as I hurried out of the room. The walls seemed to close in around me, the weight of his words pressing down on my chest. I fled to my room, closing the door behind me, as if I could shut out the reality he had just unveiled."

"The next few days passed in a haze. I threw myself into work, but every task felt mechanical, my mind never far from Arif's confession. I avoided him at all costs, dodging his attempts to talk. Each time I saw him approaching, my heart would pound, and I'd find an excuse to leave. I busied myself with trivial tasks, anything to keep my mind off the storm brewing inside me. The cold war between us became suffocating, the air icy whenever we were in the same room. My heart ached, torn between the love I had for him and the betrayal I felt deep in my bones."

"Arif didn't give up easily. He called, texted, and even left notes, each one pleading with me to talk. "Shifora, please, just let me explain." His efforts to reconcile were relentless—he showed up with coffee, flowers, my favorite pastries—yet every gesture only deepened the wound. How could he think these things could fix what had been broken?"

"At work, I could feel his eyes on me, heavy with sorrow. His colleagues noticed the tension, the way we barely spoke or even looked at each other. Yet despite the growing discomfort, Arif remained steadfast, as if he believed that time alone would mend the rift between us. But time wasn't healing anything, it only magnified the distance."

"One evening, nearly two weeks after the event, I found myself pacing in my accommodation, replaying everything in my head. I hadn't been sleeping well. Nights were restless, spent tossing and turning, replaying his words, his confession, his face twisted with regret. Every time I tried to push the thoughts away, they came back stronger, tugging at the frayed edges of my heart."

"I stared at my phone, where his last text sat unread. *Please, Shifora, I need you to understand.* The message had been there for hours, but I hadn't been able to bring myself to open it. A part of me hated how much I missed him. Hated how, despite everything, I still cared. I wanted to be angry, to let the bitterness consume me, but it was tiring and exhausting, and I was running out of energy to keep pushing him away."

"That evening, I looked around my empty apartment. The silence was deafening, and suddenly, the anger I had clung to for the past two weeks felt hollow. What was I even holding onto anymore? The thought unsettled me. I was so tired of avoiding the conversation we both knew was inevitable."

"When his knock came at the door, I hesitated. My hand hovered over the handle, part of me wanting to ignore it like I had so many times before. But something was different tonight. There hadn't been any dramatic moment, no trigger, just an overwhelming sense of weariness. I wasn't ready to forgive him, not entirely, but I also wasn't sure I could keep holding onto the silence."

"I opened the door a crack, just enough to see him. His eyes were weary, shadows of sleepless nights etched beneath them. "Shifora, please," he said softly, his voice raw. "Just hear me out."

"I stood there for what felt like an eternity. I could see the sincerity, the desperation to make things right, and for the first time, I didn't feel anger. I just felt... tired."

"With a sigh, I stepped aside, letting him in. We sat down, and the space between us darkened with unspoken words. I didn't know what I was ready to hear, but I knew one thing, we couldn't go on like this. The silence had done enough damage."

The melted heart

"I never wanted to hurt you," Arif began, his voice soft but steady. "I thought if I could start fresh with you, I could leave my past behind. But it was wrong of me to hide it from you. You deserve better."

I stared at him, his words bouncing off the walls I had so carefully built. The calmness in his voice only fanned the flames of my anger. "Better? You think telling me this now makes anything better?" My voice was sharp, laced with the resentment I had kept bottled up for too long. "You lied, Arif. You lied by omission. You let me believe we had something real when you were hiding something this huge!"

He flinched at my words but didn't look away. "Shifora, I never meant to deceive you"

"Then what did you mean to do?" I cut him off, standing up, my emotions spiraling out of control. My hands trembled as I pointed at him, unable to contain the bitterness. "Were you just hoping I'd never find out? Or that when I did, I'd forgive you on the spot like it was nothing? Do you have any idea what it feels like to be blindsided like this?"

His face fell, but I wasn't done. The floodgates had opened, and all the hurt, confusion, and anger I had been burying over the past few weeks came crashing down like a tidal wave. "You didn't even trust me enough to tell me about your past! And now, after keeping me in the dark, you expect me to understand? To just… move on?"

Arif stood up too, his expression tense. "I didn't want you to think less of me! I thought if I could show you the person I am now, without all the baggage, you could love me for who I am, not what I've been through."

I let out a hollow laugh, shaking my head. "Love you for who you are? The person I thought I knew doesn't even exist! You made sure of that by keeping this massive part of yourself hidden from me."

His eyes darkened with frustration, and his jaw clenched. "That's not fair, Shifora. People have pasts, things they're not proud of. But that doesn't mean they're defined by them. I was trying to build something better with you, something free from all of that."

I crossed my arms, my heart pounding in my chest. "And in doing so, you built it on lies, Arif. How am I supposed to trust you now? How am I supposed to believe anything you say after this?"

The room fell into a suffocating silence. Arif ran a hand through his hair, his frustration palpable. "I've made mistakes, I admit that. But this isn't just about trust, Shifora. It's about fear. I was terrified of losing you before we even really started."

I shook my head, taking a step back, tears stinging my eyes.

"Fear doesn't justify betrayal. I've been standing here, giving you everything, thinking I knew who you were, and now… now I don't even know what we are anymore."

His face twisted with pain, but I could see him struggling to hold back his own emotions. "I'm not asking for forgiveness right now. I know I don't deserve that. But I'm asking for a chance. A chance to prove that I can be better for you, that we can still make this work."

I turned away, my chest tight with anger and hurt. His words tugged at my heart, but I wasn't ready to let go of the pain. "I don't know if I can give you that chance, Arif. Right now, all I see is the person who kept me in the dark, who let me believe in something that wasn't real. And that hurts more than anything."

His face fell, and he dropped to his knees, his voice breaking with desperation. "Please, Shifora, give me a second chance. I know I've betrayed your trust, but I love you more than anything. I'll do whatever it takes to prove my sincerity and to make things right. Please, don't walk away from us."

His plea was filled with genuine emotions, a desperate bid for redemption. At that moment, I could see the depth of his remorse. It was a turning point, and though my heart was heavy, I knew we needed to confront this together.

"I love you, Shifora," Arif continued, his voice filled with earnestness. "And I want us to move forward together."

"I ——— ————————-," the rest of the sentence was swallowed by the silence between us.

Arif reached out, taking my hand gently in his. "I understand," he murmured, his touch warm and reassuring. "Take all the time you need. I'll be waiting."

As I sat with my thoughts, grappling with the uncertainties that now colored our relationship, I knew that our journey together had taken an unexpected turn. The road ahead seemed daunting, fraught with challenges and uncertainties.

But amidst the turmoil, a glimmer of hope remained, the hope that honesty and love could prevail, that we could navigate this storm together and emerge stronger. As I looked into Arif's eyes, I knew that our love story was far from over – it was just beginning, with a new chapter waiting to be written.

Arif reached out, his hand trembling slightly as he touched mine. "I'm so sorry, Shifora," he said softly, his eyes pleading for forgiveness. "I should have told you sooner. But please, believe me when I say that I love you. I want to make things right."

"I need time," I finally replied, my voice trembling. "Time to think, to understand…"

Arif nodded slowly, his expression pained. "yes yes, for sure".

When I left the room, a wave of thoughts and emotions churned within me. I had never imagined that our journey would lead to such a moment of reckoning. The future suddenly seemed uncertain, overshadowed by the truth that had shaken the foundation of our relationship.

And amidst it all, I wondered, could love to endure such an Epiphany? Was forgiveness possible, or had trust been irreparably broken?

Arif's words echoed in my mind as I grappled with the reality of his past. "She only sucked money from me," he had said, bitterness tinged in his voice. "No compassion, no love. She never treated me well, never respected me enough."

As I processed his words, I realized that there were layers to this story, complexities that I had yet to fully grasp. The pain in Arif's voice was palpable, his wounds still raw from a marriage that had left him scarred.

But amidst the hurt and confusion, a part of me still yearned to understand, to bridge the gap that had suddenly widened between us. Could I find it in myself to forgive him? Could we rebuild what had been shaken?

As I sat alone, grappling with the burden of Arif's confession, one thing became clear, our love story had taken an unexpected turn, one that would test us in ways we had never imagined.

That night, I reconsidered everything. Yet, with a reassuring tone, Arif promised me that the divorce from his first marriage would be final in a day or two, and it would all be over. But as they say, "pyaar andha hota hai" (love is blind) in my case, it was deaf too. If this were an Indian teledrama, we could have filled an hour-long episode with this exposition, and my reaction, yes, it was that dramatic.

Later that night, I thought it was over. That night, I had a nightmare. I saw Arif, dressed impeccably as a groom, but lying in a coffin. I woke up in a bad mood but kept this to myself until now. Now you know it too.

Sid looked Shifora straight in the eyes, his expression questioning, "So you canceled the wedding?"

Shifora met his gaze head-on and without hesitation replied firmly, "Yet, I was so deeply in love that I assured him I wouldn't leave him."

Sid let out a disapproving sound, "Pfft… why didn't you? You had a very good chance here," he interrupted.

Shifora said, "It wasn't easy to call it off. I had already canceled one engagement in the past when I was much younger in my teens. I faced consequences and shamed my family back then, and no one apart from my father had supported me. Now that they all have accepted me, I didn't want to repeat the same, so I held to my decision."

Sid's expressions soured. His downturned lips and furrowed brow spoke volumes, revealing the depth of his frustration and disillusionment. "So, it was your fear of canceling another marriage and facing your family that overshadowed what was glaringly evident before you?"

"We all deserve second chances in life, Sid. Sometimes, we

cling to hope because it's easier to hold on to the possibility of redemption than to face the harsh reality of our decisions. Shifora responded in defense.

"Okay, so now I get how you and Arif crossed paths, but what about the rest? How did the marriage preparations unfold? I'm curious about the whole journey. How did your love story evolve from meeting to tying the knot? Was it as dreamy and perfect as it sounds?"

Twenty-Five

Marriage preps in Goa

"Well, now that I've heard your pre-marital not-so-rosy story," Sid said with a hint of sarcasm, "I'm a bit more intrigued. What about after the wedding? What happened there? Shadi ke baad kya kya hua? (what happens after marriage)."

Shifora's eyes narrowed slightly, a smirk playing at her lips. "Oh, shadi ke baad nahi," (not only after marriage) she replied with a knowing look, "Shadi ke dauran bhi bohot kuch hua. (many things happened during the marriage too)"

"In the days leading up to my return to Goa, the anticipation was palpable. My family was buzzing with excitement, ready to welcome me back with a mix of joy and a thousand questions. The news of our impending marriage had spread like wildfire, reaching even the most distant relatives and old friends. "

"Upon returning to Goa, I dove headfirst into wedding

planning. I tackled invite lists and to-do lists, but planning our inter-country, inter-faith marriage proved tricky. Online research was a dead end, and I felt overwhelmed."

"I sought advice from our Church priest, hoping to get some clarity on how to navigate the marriage preparations," Shifora began, her voice steady as she recounted the memories. "Father Joseph was kind and understanding, offering guidance for the church ceremony. He emphasized the importance of a strong spiritual foundation and suggested bringing Arif along for the next visit."

She paused, a small smile playing on her lips as she remembered. "Father Joseph even joked about how Arif would need to brush up on his biblical knowledge. It was a lighthearted moment, but it didn't prepare me for the bureaucratic maze that lay ahead." Sid raised his eyebrow and tweaked his lips as if suppressing disbelief.

Shifora's expression darkened as she continued. "Here's where it got tricky. We needed to have a court marriage first, but when we went to the court, they said we needed church registration. So, we went back to the church, but they insisted we needed court approval first. It was like being caught in a never-ending loop, each side passing the buck."

She leaned forward, her frustration evident. "I felt like a ball getting kicked around, bouncing from one authority to another. Each visit to the court or church was met with more paperwork, more signatures, and more confusion. The whole process felt deliberately convoluted as if they were testing our resolve."

Shifora sighed, shaking her head. "I remember one particular day when we had all the required documents, or so we thought. We stood in line at the court for hours, only to be told that one of the forms was outdated. The clerk looked at us with such indifference, as if our struggle meant nothing. I felt a surge of anger, but also a sense of helplessness. It was exhausting, physically and emotionally."

She glanced at Sid, what she saw there was a mixture of empathy and authentic inquisitiveness. "Arif tried to stay positive, always reassuring me that we'd get through it. But there were moments when even he seemed to falter. It was a constant back and forth, a relentless tug-of-war that wore us down."

Twenty-Six

Signs of the Universe

"Love is not a feeling. Love is an action, an activity. Genuine love implies commitment and the exercise of wisdom, and it always involves a personal decision."
— M. Scott Peck, *The Road Less Traveled*

Shifora took a deep breath. "It wasn't just about getting the approvals. It felt like our commitment was being tested at every step. Through it all, I had to keep my family in the dark, knowing they wouldn't understand why we had to go through such an ordeal. It was supposed to be a joyous time, but instead, it felt like we were fighting a battle just to be together."

"I urged Arif to get his family involved, especially since his parents were needed to sign as witnesses," Shifora continued, her voice tinged with concern. "But Arif kept saying they would come closer to the date. Shifora looked at Arif, concern evident in her eyes. "Arif, are you sure about all this? We need to finalize everything soon."

Arif shrugged, his tone nonchalant. "Don't worry, Shifora. We've got plenty of time. It'll all come together."

Her worry deepened. "But we still have so many details to sort out. We can't just leave everything to the last minute."

Arif seemingly unfazed. "Relax, it'll be fine. Trust me."

She leaned back, her eyes reflecting the anxiety of those days. "I tried to understand his perspective, thinking maybe it was a cultural difference or perhaps his parents were genuinely busy. But as the days passed, the pressure started to mount. My family was already skeptical about the interfaith marriage, and this delay only added to their doubts."

Shifora's fingers tapped nervously on the table as she re-counted the events. "I remember one evening, after another fruitless conversation with the court officials, I called Arif. My voice was strained, almost pleading. 'Arif, we need your parents here. The court won't move forward without their signatures. We're running out of time.'"

She sighed, the memory still vivid. "Arif reassured me, as he always did, but there was a hint of hesitation in his voice that I couldn't ignore. 'They'll be here, Shifora,' he said. 'Just a few more days.' But those days felt like an eternity."

Her gaze dropped to the floor, her voice softer. "I started to feel a creeping sense of dread. What if they didn't show up? What if this was all a sign that things were falling apart? Every delay, every postponement felt like another obstacle in our path, testing our patience and our commitment."

Shifora looked up, her eyes meeting Sid's. "There were nights I couldn't sleep, my mind racing with worst-case scenarios. I kept picturing the disappointment in my parents' eyes, and the whispers of doubt from friends and family. It was a weight that grew heavier with each passing day."

She took a deep breath, steadying herself. "Despite my fears, I tried to stay strong. I kept pushing Arif, reminding him of the deadlines, and the importance of his parents' presence. But every time he said 'soon,' I felt a little more of my resolve slip away."

Shifora's voice wavered slightly as she finished. "It wasn't just about the signatures. It was about feeling supported, knowing that both our families were behind us. But in those moments, I felt very much alone, fighting a battle that seemed to grow more daunting by the day."

Twenty-Seven

Arif's arrival to Goa

"Arif came to Goa and stayed in a nearby inn, preparing for the wedding while we navigated the bureaucratic hurdles together.

Back then, Arif didn't know how to ride a bike. Whenever we needed to run errands or go anywhere, I insisted he sit behind me as we rode. My mother wasn't entirely pleased with this arrangement, but my stubbornness left her with little choice. It was our little rebellion against tradition, and it felt oddly liberating.

One day, my mother, in a rare moment of attempting to bridge the gap, asked Arif, "Shouldn't you learn to ride? It would make things so much easier for both of you."

Arif, with his usual nonchalance, replied, "Why would I learn that? We don't need it back on my island; it's a waste of time."

My mother frowned slightly, trying to understand. "But you're here now, in Goa. It would be helpful, don't you think?"

Arif shook his head dismissively. "I don't see the point. Shifora manages just fine. It's not something I'll ever need."

Her eyes widened slightly, confusion giving way to concern. "But what about when she's not around? It's important to be self-sufficient, Arif."

Arif shrugged, clearly uninterested. "We'll cross that bridge when we get there."

My mother's lips pressed into a thin line, her thoughts racing. I could almost see the confirmation of her fears that I had made a wrong choice etched clearly on her face.

Of course, the comments from others weren't always kind. "Anvoi, teka bike chalupa pasun koina?" they would say, which translates to, "What a shame, he doesn't even know how to ride a bike? In our place, even the 12-year-old boys ride a bike nowadays, just that it's not legal yet. But for Arif, growing up on the islands meant he never had much use for a bike. There were no roads there. The Islands were small, hence no use of the roads either.

"Arif's stature only added to the spectacle. He was tall and heavyset, while I looked like a mere puppy in comparison. Yet despite the whispers and stares, I was determined to stand by him, bike or no bike."

Sid grinned and replied, "Sounds like a comedy show waiting to happen! You two must have been quite the sight cruising around on that bike."

Shifora giggled and continued.

"Before weddings in the Roman Catholic tradition, there are certain formalities to complete, and one of them is completing a wedding course. Now, don't imagine this as a daunting task with a big fat textbook and exams like NEET. Instead, it's a series of sessions where they teach you about married life and how to navigate it as husband and wife."

"Normally, the course spans several weeks, but ours was fast-tracked due to the complexities of our international and interfaith marriage. Each session involved the priest routinely asking if anyone had forced us into the marriage, ensuring it was a conscious decision on both sides. We would nod eagerly, our responses betraying just a hint of nervous urgency. Looking back, I'm certain the priest could sense that mixture of excitement and anxiety in our answers a reflection of the storm we were caught up in

As the course drew to a close, we found ourselves amidst a gale of emotions. The sessions had been intense, filled with introspective questions and deep conversations. Despite the rushed pace and underlying anxiety, there was an undeniable sense of clarity emerging from the chaos."

"Our last session arrived, and as we left the church, hand in hand, a feeling of quiet determination settled over us. The priest's final blessing was a comforting reminder of the sacred commitment we were about to make."

"Walking away from the church, I took a deep breath, letting the weight of the past few weeks sink in. We had faced our fears, navigated the complexities of our unique situation, and emerged more certain of our path together. The journey had not been easy, but it had brought us closer, reinforcing the bond we were about to formalize."

"Looking at Arif, I saw not just a partner but someone who had weathered the storm with me. The challenges we faced had only made us stronger, and as we prepared for our wedding, I felt a renewed sense of hope and excitement for the future. We were not just preparing for a ceremony but embarking on a shared journey, one built on understanding, respect, and an unwavering commitment to each other."

"With each step we took, I realized that while the road ahead might be unpredictable, we were ready to face it together, fortified by the lessons learned and the love that had carried us through. The future was ours to shape, and as we looked ahead, I felt a sense of anticipation for the life we were about to build."

Twenty-Eight

The never-ending Marriage preps

"Meanwhile, back at home, all the wedding preparations were in full swing. Wedding preparations are nothing less than a circus, and at my wedding, I was more of a clown and less of a bride. A clown who was running pillar to post to arrange everything and nurturing the illusion of being the ringmaster."

"My mother had her ideas about how things should be done. She vetoed my choice of wedding reception venue, and the band, and even refused to allow videography at the wedding. Each veto felt like a personal affront, a dismissal of my dreams and desires. I remember the sting of disappointment when she casually dismissed the venue I had set my heart on, the place where I had imagined so many beautiful moments unfolding. The band I adored was replaced with one she deemed more appropriate, their songs devoid of the emotions I wanted to share on my special day."

"When she flatly refused videography, I felt a pang of heartbreak. I had wanted to capture every moment, to preserve the memories in a way that could be revisited and cherished. Instead, it felt like she was erasing the narrative I had hoped to create. Each decision she overturned was a small wound, and amidst the flurry of wedding preparations, these wounds began to accumulate, leaving me feeling more and more disconnected from the celebration that was supposed to be about Arif and me. The tension between honoring my mother's wishes and staying true to my vision of our wedding created a silent but powerful undercurrent of frustration and sadness."

"Arif, unfamiliar with the customs and tasks at hand, often found himself comfortably seated on the sofa, leaving my dad and me to brainstorm and tackle the endless list of arrangements. From booking the catering and the wedding venue to inviting guests and managing countless other tasks, I needed his help, but he remained a passive observer, physically present or actionally uninvolved."

"Frustration simmered within me, but I didn't want to make a scene. Dad, sensing the tension, gave me a reassuring look before taking a seat beside me at the dining table, where endless lists and brochures were scattered."

"He placed a warm hand on my shoulder. "I've got your back, Shifora. You'll never have to carry this alone."

"Thanks, Dad," I sighed, grateful for his steady presence.

Without missing a beat, he picked up one of the folders. "Let's tackle this venue booking first. Between the two of us, we can get this sorted by tomorrow."

"As I watched him study the details, his strong, quiet determination washed over me, giving me the strength I needed. He was the rock that never faltered, the one person who showed up with both hands ready to work, even when others didn't."

Dad glanced up with a glint of mischief. "And if that's not enough, you know I've got a mean glare reserved just for lazy bystanders."

I smirked, and my mood lifted.

"Amidst the chaos of preparations, the looming pressure of incomplete legal and church formalities added an extra layer of stress. To add to the complications, Arif's mother fell ill and was unable to travel to Goa for our wedding. You see another sign from the Universe. My mother voiced her doubts, "Has she accepted you or not?"

I looked down, unable to meet her gaze. "She… she said she wanted to come. It's just… bad timing, I guess."

My mother's eyes narrowed, not convinced. "Bad timing or…?"

I swallowed hard, my voice barely a whisper. "I don't know, Mom. Maybe it's just too much for her right now."

She sighed, shaking her head. "Shifora, you can't keep making excuses. It feels like everything is falling apart."

I couldn't bring myself to respond, the weight of her words pressing heavily on my heart.

Despite her reservations, I chose to ignore her concerns and continued with the plans. By now you would have realized that our parents never even met once before our marriage to discuss it.

"Till the last day, I was still unsure if the wedding would take place or not. Sid's heart ached while listening to all this and somewhere deep down amidst this ache, the hope was still breathing shallow."

Twenty-Nine

Thickening preps of marriage

"Wait, hold on a second," Sid interrupted, his brow furrowing with further doubts. "If your parents never met, how did they react when they finally did?"

Shifora paused, her hand hovering over the plate of french fries. She looked up at Sid, looked at the plate of fries again, picked up one fry, and said "Oh, Sid, you have no idea. It was... an experience, to say the least."

Sid was intrigued. "An experience? Do tell."

Shifora sighed, trying to munch on the fry she had just taken a bite of. "Well, imagine this. My parents are traditional and very set in their ways. Arif's family, on the other hand, was much more laid-back, almost indifferent.

Shifora paced around the living room, checking her watch every few minutes. "I'm starting to get anxious, Arif. Your father and brother have just arrived, and it's been a bit chaotic with all the last-minute planning. What if the hotel isn't comfortable? And where are your friends? You mentioned they were coming too."

Arif walked over and gently placed a hand on her shoulder. "Hey, breathe. Everything is going to be okay. We've made sure your father and brother have a comfortable place to stay. I called the hotel earlier, and they assured me everything is set."

Shifora sighed, still looking worried. "But what about your friends? You said they were supposed to come too."

Arif gave her a reassuring smile. "Yeah, I did mention them. They were supposed to arrive, but they haven't shown up yet. They might still join us later. Sometimes things don't go exactly as planned, but we'll manage. The most important thing is that we're all together now and that everyone is settled."

Shifora looked at him, a little reassured but still tense. "I hope you're right. I just want everything to go smoothly."

Arif squeezed her shoulder gently. "I'm sure it will. We've got this. Let's focus on enjoying the time we have and making the best of it. We can't control everything, but we can handle whatever comes our way together."

Shifora nodded, taking a deep breath. "Okay, you're right. Thanks for calming me down."

Arif pulled her into a comforting hug. "Anytime. Let's make the most of this moment. Everything will fall into place."

Sid raised an eyebrow, his tone of suspicion. "In a family with three brothers, three sisters, and parents, only his father and younger brother showed up. Did you find that odd?"

Shifora gave a wry smile on her lips. "Odd? No, not really. You see, love isn't just blind; it's also deaf and mute. Every time someone suggested that something might be off, I'd only deepen my delusions, layering on new excuses and wrapping myself in a fabric of toxic positivity."

Sid looked at her, intrigued by her candidness. "So you're saying you chose to ignore the red flags?"

Shifora nodded, her expression thoughtful. "Exactly. I was so wrapped up in my idealized version of things that I kept convincing myself that everything was fine, even when it wasn't."

Sid looked at Shifora and smirked, "Ah, the plot thickens! It's like we're in a suspense thriller, but with more family drama and less action. What do you make of this family dynamics, Shifora?"

Shifora replied shaking her head in amusement. "I know, right? It's like I was living in a Bollywood movie without even realizing it! Who knew wedding planning could be this entertaining?"

When they finally met, it was like watching two completely different worlds collide."

Sid raised an eyebrow. "Sounds like a recipe for disaster."

Shifora nodded. "It was tense. My mother, with her piercing questions and disapproving looks. It was awkward, to say the least."

Sid grinned, trying to lighten the mood. "So, did anyone throw a punch?"

"No punches, thankfully. But the glares were sharp enough to cut through steel. They wanted everything to be as simple and streamlined as possible, just one step and done. But we were determined to follow each ceremony to the letter. It didn't go smoothly at all. It took a lot of effort to get through that lunch without anyone walking out. Let's just say the tension was thick enough to slice through." Shifora laughed.

"We lived in a rented house those days. Our landlord was quite fond of me, treating me like her own and proudly introducing me as her friend. But the moment she learned about my relationship with an interfaith guy, she distanced herself faster than you could say awkward."

Sid said sarcastically. "Sounds like she upgraded you from friend to frenemy real quick."

Shifora giggled, nodding in agreement. "Exactly. It was like I got demoted from bestie to blacklisted in her books overnight."

To make matters worse, she couldn't attend the wedding as she lost her brother just a day before the big day. "Talk about a plot twist," Shifora remarked, torn between feeling happy or sad about her absence.

Sid leaned back, contemplating. "Sounds like a scene straight out of a soap opera. But hey, every good story needs a little drama, right?"

Shifora sighed. "True, but when it's your own life, it's hard to figure out if it's a sign from the universe or just plain bad luck."

Thirty

A Night before the marriage

"It was the night before our wedding, and the air was thick with anticipation. At my place, we held a Rose ceremony, a Traditional Catholic ritual akin to the Haldi ceremony in other parts of India."

"After the ceremony, tradition dictated that we were not allowed to meet or interact until the nuptials, as it was considered unlucky. Even leaving our homes was forbidden to protect us from evil spirits. Since Arif was unfamiliar with this tradition, my distant relatives visited his hotel and completed the ritual for him, which touched him deeply."

"The Roce ceremony transitioned into a joyous atmosphere of celebration with the traditional "Rocache Jevon" or feast. Everyone was in high spirits, celebrating the upcoming union with food, music, and laughter."

"The night before the wedding was anything but restful. It was past midnight by the time we finally settled into bed, only to be jolted awake by the buzzing of my phone at 4 am. It was the decoration team at the church, followed swiftly by the arrival of makeup artists and other vendors."

Sid grinned, "Wow, 4 am chaos and a full-blown vendor invasion? Did you accidentally sign up for a wedding or a live reality show?"

Shifora with a tired smile on her face. "It felt like both, Sid. I was ready to hand out trophies for 'Best Chaos Coordinator' and 'Most Patient Bride' if only I could find the time between the madness."

"Just as I was ready to unravel from the early morning chaos, dad swooped in, organizing the crowd with his usual calm authority. I watched as he gathered the sleepy, groggy-eyed relatives and friends, patting them on the back and handing out quick pep talks as though they were gearing up for a marathon."

"All right, everyone!" he called, his voice steady but firm, cutting through the chatter. "Let's get moving—we've got a wedding to pull off here! Kids, stay close to your parents, and the rest, follow me! Buses are parked outside, and we're heading to the church."

There was something infectious about his energy, his enthusiasm sparking even the most reluctant into action. He moved through the crowd, checking on the vendors, reassuring the elders, and helping anyone who seemed a little lost. With each nod and gesture, I could feel his pride and support lifting my spirits.

As the last of the relatives shuffled outside, dad turned to me, a smile full of warmth lighting his face. "You've got this, Shifora. And we're all here with you, every step of the way."

"His words settled in my heart like an anchor, grounding

me amid the frenzy. As he led the group out, his voice echoing with encouragement and direction, I felt an overwhelming gratitude. He wasn't just my father; he was my rock, my silent cheerleader, carrying everyone forward when I needed it the most."

The next few hours were a storm of activities, with kids running around, elders bustling about, and chaos reigning supreme.

"According to tradition, the groom's family sends a team to prepare the bride for the wedding. They handle everything from makeup to dresses, symbolizing the groom's intention to welcome her into his life. But in my case, it felt more like going through the motions without any real meaning attached. After all, I had chosen this path, hadn't I? At that moment, it didn't feel any different."

"Despite the lack of personal significance, the blessings ceremony proceeded as per tradition, and soon we were all on our way to the church."

Thirty-One

At the Church

"Yay! She said yes!" a voice rang out from the other side of the café, sparking applause and laughter.

Shifora and Sid glanced over to see a young woman beaming, her hands covering her mouth in disbelief, as her fiancé stood up, pulling her into a hug. Friends around them clapped and cheered, some wiping away tears, while the newly engaged couple basked in the joy of the moment.

Sid leaned back, grinning. "It's like a movie scene," he mused, watching the couple as they showed off the ring to an admiring group of friends. "I guess there's something about popping the question that just makes everyone feel like they're part of it."

Shifora nodded, her smile softening as she watched the couple. "There's a certain magic to it, isn't there?" she said. "The nerves, the thrill, that burst of happiness…"

Sid glanced at her thoughtfully, catching a hint of nostalgia in her eyes. He took a sip of his coffee, then leaned in a bit closer. "So… speaking of big moments… what was your wedding day like?"

Shifora with warmth in her expression mingling with a touch of longing. "Oh, that day…. my friends and I arrived right on time, but as usual, the groom's side was fashionably late. The priest was rushing things too, which got my parents all worked up. After a flurry of calls and follow-ups, they finally arrived, claiming there had been an accident on the way."

Sid's eyes widened in mock horror. "An accident?"

Shifora said with a tinge of exasperation in her voice. "Maybe so. It felt like the universe was auditioning for its drama series, with me as the reluctant lead. Do you think this was yet another sign from the universe?"

"In the church tradition, the groom is supposed to arrive first, eagerly awaiting his bride. It's a symbolic gesture of his readiness to welcome her into his life. When the bride arrives, the best man traditionally offers her a bouquet, gives her a kiss on the cheek to welcome her into their family, and then covers her face with a veil before formally handing her over to the groom. Together, they stand outside the church entrance, where the priest blesses them and leads them inside, symbolically guiding them towards God."

"However, on our wedding day, nerves were running high as minutes turned into anxious anticipation. None of these traditional rituals could take place. Instead, we were hastily blessed by the priest before rushing down the aisle, eager to begin our journey together as husband and wife."

"The arrival of Arif's family at the church was straight out of "Men in Black," decked out in black suits and sunglasses. It was a sight to behold, one that my friends still tease me about to this day. The contrast between their attire and the solemn church setting added an unexpected touch of humor, making it a memorable moment amidst the nerves and excitement of the day. Sid's laughter rang out, hearty and infectious, "I mean, who walks into the church with the sunglasses on." soon Shifora joined in."

After a while, their laughter subsided, and they collected themselves. "And then?" Sid asked eagerly, his tone laced with anticipation, eager to hear the continuation of Shifora's wedding day.

"The nuptials continued as normal. During the ring exchange ceremony, one of the rings fell not once, but twice, rolling towards my mother. Once is a coincidence, but what about the second time? Was it the universe intervening again, or perhaps a loved one from heaven trying to stop me from making a mistake?

Either way, we didn't stop. One of my close friends, Jennifer in Goa, signed a witness for me followed by some other relatives in the church, and finally, we were married and announced husband and wife."

As Shifora recited these words, Sid, on the verge of controlling his frustration, broke the glass of water he was holding on the table. His tears flowed freely as he uttered, "What have you done to yourself, Shifora?"

The question sounded familiar, but before Shifora could recollect, she saw Sid's hand was bleeding and hurriedly rushed to the counter to check for first aid. She cleaned the wound on Sid's hand and completed the first aid. Simultaneously, the staff from the cafe cleared the broken glass. There was a screaming silence between them, naturally, Sid did not expect any answer.

After a moment, Shifora, feeling the weight of the silence, gently suggested, "Sid, let's move to another table." She gestured towards a quieter corner of the cafe, away from the remnants of the broken glass and the lingering tension.

Sid nodded in agreement, silently following Shifora to the quieter corner of the cafe. They settled into their new seats, the atmosphere slightly less charged but still heavy with unspoken words. Shifora sighed softly, breaking the silence that hung between them.

"I didn't mean to upset you, Sid," she began, her voice filled with concern as she looked at his hand, now bandaged. "I just… I needed to tell someone, and I thought you would understand."

Sid gave a small nod, his face showing he got it. "I'm sorry for how I acted, Shifora," he said, looking down at the table. "I didn't mean to make things tough."

"It's okay,"

He looked up at her, giving a half-smile. "I want to understand, Shifora. I just… worry about you. You're like a walking soap opera, and I'm here for every dramatic twist," he admitted, his tone light and playful.

"I know, Sid," she said sincerely. She said cheerfully.

Thirty-Two

The Blessings After Wedding

'They sat in silence for a moment, the tension easing as they collected their thoughts. Eventually, Sid broke the quiet again with a tentative smile. "So, what happened next?" he asked gently, steering the conversation back to Shifora's story.'

"You know, Sid, even up to that moment, I didn't feel like I was married. It was as if I was running and rushing through everything," Shifora reflected, her voice tinged with a hint of sadness. "I couldn't fully enjoy or immerse myself in the rituals and traditions of the wedding. I was physically present, but mentally ……….?."

"Are you okay Shifora, do you want to continue" Sid acknowledged, his gaze warm and understanding. "Weddings can be like that, especially with all the expectations and traditions."

"Exactly," Shifora agreed, her voice filled with a mix of

emotions. "I wanted to enjoy it, to feel the significance of each ritual, but it all happened so quickly."

"Anyways, it was a reality. After the nuptials, as per tradition, the married couple stands at the entrance of the church so that everyone can queue up to bless them as a couple. Everyone wished them well and proceeded to the designated venue for the reception. While we waited for everyone to move, we stayed back at the church for some photoshoots. My friends Rebecca and Jennifer were with me at that moment.

"We were still at the church, in the middle of the photo shoot, when we got the news that the priest who celebrated our nuptials had met with an accident."

"This was the first time I didn't feel right about things," Shifora said, her brow furrowing.

"Was he hurt bad?" interrupted Sid, concern evident in his voice.

"Not much, just a slight bruise on the head, that's what I was told" Shifora replied, trying to downplay the situation. "Before I could start getting worried about it, my friends swooped in like a storm of wedding preparation."

"Don't worry about that now, Shifora. We need to finalize the seating arrangements and check if the DJ has arrived," Rebecca said, taking Shifora's hand and leading her away from the conversation.

"Yeah, we've got this. Let's focus on making sure everyone has a good time," Jennifer chimed in, giving Shifora a reassuring smile.

Sid leaned forward, eyes narrowing slightly as he caught the shift in Shifora's tone. "But it wasn't just that, was it? You said this was the first time you didn't feel right about things. What do you mean?"

Shifora hesitated, her fingers nervously tracing the rim of her coffee cup. Her eyes flickered as if replaying the moment in her mind. "It's hard to explain. There was something…off, something I couldn't shake. It wasn't just the priest's accident or the rush of the day. It was like a shadow hanging over me, something I didn't want to acknowledge."

Sid's brow furrowed, concern deepening. "A shadow?"

Shifora nodded slowly, the weight of the memory settling in the air between them. "As we left for the reception, there was this sense of…foreboding. I don't know, Sid. Maybe I was just overwhelmed. But even now, thinking back, I can't help but wonder if that was the moment everything started to unravel."

At Reception

"**Kit re tumi? Time choi tumgelo? Itu late mhun jevonn dovortai?**" one of the guests at the reception hall shouted angrily, his voice cutting through the crowd. ("What's wrong with you people? Do you have no respect for our time? Who keeps lunch this late?")

His frustration was palpable, and as he continued, a string of curses followed.

My father, along with a few other guests, quickly stepped in, trying to calm him down.

"Sorry sorry, it's just a slight delay. Everything's almost ready," my father reassured, his voice steady despite the situation.

But the man only huffed, folding his arms. "Time choi tumgelo! We've all waiting here for ages! It's no way to treat guests."

Dad met his gaze, undeterred by the guest's outburst. "Yes, I understand," he replied gently, lowering his voice as he leaned in, his tone both respectful and unyielding. "But think about it, this is a once-in-a-lifetime day for our families. A few more minutes won't hurt, will it?"

"The guest's scowl softened, his shoulders relaxing slightly. My father had a genuine smile that seemed to ease the tension even further. 'Soon we'll all be eating, drinking, celebrating together, just a little late. But isn't it worth the wait?"

After a moment, the man nodded reluctantly, grumbling under his breath but pacified. Dad patted his shoulder with a chuckle, "And besides, we saved the best food for you!"

"With that, the guest cracked a small smile, the anger dissipating as dad led him back toward his seat, nodding to a few others to settle down as well. As he turned back to me, his eyes met mine, offering a quick wink. In that brief exchange, he reassured me once again he had everything under control, and that he'd carry the weight of the world on his shoulders."

But the damage had already been done, the restlessness had started to spread through the crowd like a ripple, and the uneasy energy overpowered the environment.

Sid's gaze never wavered, his voice low but steady. "That means... that shadow...?" He let the words trail off, the silence finishing what he didn't need to say.

Shifora met his eyes, her expression unreadable. Slowly, she nodded, unspoken memories settling between them like a heavy fog.

"What happened after that?" Sid asked softly, his eagerness mixed with a quiet understanding.

"In Goa, it's customary to raise a toast with wine or champagne at Christian weddings. When it came time to open the champagne, I envisioned a glamorous moment, with corks popping and bubbly flowing. Instead, it was more like a scene from a comedy sketch. The cork went rogue, and the champagne splashed onto the unsuspecting family members standing nearby, including Arif's father. Imagine his face like he'd just been told his favorite football team had lost the finals. He was visibly upset, probably thinking we had a hidden agenda to soak him, which caused tension and discomfort among the guests."

"In hindsight, I should have given everyone a heads-up about the alcohol being served. Arif's father was so disappointed that he decided to give me and my mother the silent treatment for the rest of the day. Great, just what I needed another thing to feel guilty about. As if that wasn't enough, a distant uncle, who had moonlighted as a drill sergeant in a past life, began yelling about the arrangements. He was like an angry orchestra conductor waving his arms and barking orders, which only added to the chaos and discomfort."

"Typically, wedding receptions in Goa are a vortex of music and dance performances, with everyone joining in to celebrate. But at ours? Crickets. Not a soul came forward to dance. It was as if the dance floor was made of hot lava. I felt like a party planner whose guests had all RSVP'd "No." Unworthy and disheartened."

"Amidst these disappointments, we received a call from the hotel where my in-laws were staying, informing us of a flight rescheduling. Because, of course, what's a wedding without a little last-minute chaos? Despite the rush, we decided it was best for them to leave. Unfortunately, even by that time, Arif's father remained distant and unapproachable, like he was auditioning for a role in a silent film. Due to the rush caused by the flight changes, the tradition of formally handing over the daughter to the husband was skipped, which upset my mother even more. She had been looking forward to that moment, and now it was just another thing on the growing list of wedding mishaps."

"Picture a room full of people who had all just realized they left their ovens on at home. It was an overwhelming day filled with mixed emotions. I found it difficult to stay present in the moment, my mind racing and unable to find space to breathe. It was like being in a well-meaning chaos, and I was just trying to keep my feet on the ground."

Sid questioned, "So, was the wedding over?"

"No, it wasn't over yet," Shifora said with a weary smile as if describing a marathon that, despite crossing the halfway mark, still stretched endlessly ahead.

"As per tradition, after the marriage and reception, the bride normally goes to the groom's home. In my case, we went to my home instead. We had some intimate family functions there."

"The house was full of relatives, with talk, music, laughter, and cheers filling every corner. It seemed like everyone had forgotten the mishaps of the reception. My mother had arranged and gifted a gold chain to Arif, which she had managed to organize secretly using my brother's funds. It's a tradition for the bride's family to give a gold chain to the groom, but I wasn't aware of this until it happened with Arif."

"As all the activities of the day came to an end, we were surrounded by relatives and friends, the air buzzing with exhaustion and relief. I took a moment to glance at everyone while I was seated among them. The day had been a chaotic blur, and despite the signs, I had convinced myself that everything would eventually fall into place."

"Then, as my eyes met my mother's face across the room, a sinking feeling took hold of me. It wasn't just her tired, strained smile or the exhaustion etched into her features that struck me. It was the jibes I overheard from a few family members, their voices laced with criticism, as they commented on how she had looked "defeated" and "as if she had given up on her dreams for her daughter's sake.""

"The realization hit me like a tidal wave. Until that moment, I had been blindfolded by hope and stubbornness, unable to see the unfolding disaster. The look on my mother's face, coupled with the biting remarks of those around me, shattered the illusion I had been living in. I felt as if I had not just made a mistake but had orchestrated a calamity, an undeniable signal from the universe that I had ignored until it was almost too late."

"Did she look angry?" Sid interrupted.

"No, she was not angry," Shifora replied, her voice softening.

Sid leaned in closer, his fascination stirred. "Then what was it? Disappointment? Sadness?"

Shifora sighed, her gaze distant. "It was deeper. The kind

that mothers have when they know their child is about to do something wrong. It was as if she knew the road ahead would be hard for me, but she couldn't say anything more. Her silence spoke volumes.

A moment of silence passed between them, filled with unspoken empathy and connection. Then Sid broke it with a gentle, "So, what happened next?"

Thirty-Four

The Guilt

"You know, Mrs. Dias, her daughter Shifora married that boy from the island. I heard his family didn't even bother to come. It's a shame. Such a prestigious family, reduced to this."

"The words cut through the air like a blade, sharp and cold. Mrs. Shirwaikar, notorious for her razor-edged tongue, stood near the doorway, her voice dripping with judgment. She leaned in closer to another guest, her eyes gleaming with the kind of delight only gossip can ignite."

"I stood frozen in the corner, unseen but not unheard, as the conversation twisted like a knife in my gut. The laughter that followed felt hollow, echoing through the walls of my home, a place that once felt safe but now felt foreign."

"That day, I realized some shadows come from people, not events. And the wedding wasn't just the beginning of my new life; it was the beginning of being judged by everyone in it."

"At that moment, the weight of my decisions crashed down on me. The whispers, the snide remarks, the blatant gossip all of it suddenly felt like a storm raging around me, with my mother at its eye, enduring it all with silent resilience. Her silent endurance, her eyes filled with unshed tears, broke something inside me. It was as if I could finally see the invisible burden she had been carrying because of my choices. It was then that I realized, I had not just made mistakes; I had dragged my family into a quagmire of societal disdain and personal disappointment. And the worst part? I had been too blind to see it until that very moment."

Shifora paused, her voice breaking. "It was a wave of realization that flushed over me. As tears rolled down my cheeks and to avoid breaking down in front of all my relatives and friends, I… I yelled at my mother. Yes, I yelled at her, saying, 'Why are you doing this?' The room went pin-drop silent. No one knew what had happened, and neither could we explain it to anyone. How rude and disrespectful I was, "wasn't I?"

Shifora looked down, a mix of shame and regret on her face. "This is the guilt I carried for all those years until I was healed. No mother asks anything from their child, except love. But here, she did not ask even for that. However, what she was asking, was to stand up for myself. And that was the only thing I was not ready to give her at that moment.

Sid was feeling Heartbroken, feeling the weight of Shifora's guilt. Trying to lighten the mood a bit, he said, "Well, if it's any consolation, I'm sure I've been yelled at by my mom more times than I can count. And I probably deserved it every time."

Shifora gleed, the tension easing a little. "Mothers do have that special way of putting us back on track, don't they?"

Sid nodded a faint smile on his lips. "Absolutely. And they always manage to do it with love, no matter how tough the situation," he said, glancing at Shifora. "I've seen your mom do it too. Remember that time she convinced you to take that gap year? She knew exactly what you needed before you did."

After a brief silence, Shifora continued, her voice trembling, "I thought to myself, what have I done? Have I spoiled everything? My relationship with my parents, friends, neighbors, and parish. Have I ruined Arif's life too? All this while, I was confident that I would make it happen, make a life with Arif, but this invisible slap hurt hard."

Shifora wept as she said this, her emotions overwhelming her. She was unable to say anything more, her sobs filling the space between them. Sid, unsure of how to react, got out of his chair and came closer to Shifora. Sid didn't know what to do, he knelt halfway beside her, his voice gentle and soothing as he assured her, he fidgeted awkwardly, glancing around the room. Hesitantly, he reached for a tissue from the table and handed it to her, his voice soft and uncertain, "I... I'm with you."

Shifora thought for a moment, her tears slowing as she pondered, Shifora looked up at Sid, her eyes red and swollen. As she took the tissue, a thought crossed her mind: "Is he for real? She glanced at Sid, his face filled with concern and empathy.

This reminded Shifora of a quote from a book: "You are the best friend" by Ajay K Pandey, it said. " The person who sympathizes would say, "We are always with you" and the one who loves you will say "I am always with you".

Thirty-Five

Married but not Married

"Sid remained by her side, offering silent support as Shifora wrestled with her thoughts and feelings. The warmth of his presence and the sincerity of his words provided a much-needed balm to her wounded heart. The connection between them, though not yet fully formed, began to take root, offering Shifora a glimmer of solace in her pain."

Sid leaned in, his eagerness palpable. "How did you handle your emotions at that time, Shifora?

Shifora sighed, gathering her thoughts. "Well, the day ended with some quality time spent with our family, friends, and relatives. Arif seemed blissfully unaware of the turmoil brewing inside me, while I felt exhausted and on the verge of crankiness, longing for nothing more than to retreat to bed."

Arif had used an employee benefit to book two rooms at the Taj Exotica Resorts and Spa in Benaulim, Goa. After our eventful day, we planned to spend two days there before returning home, as the resort was conveniently located an hour away from our house. We had arranged for a cab to drop us off, arriving at the resort close to 11 pm.

"Navigating through the lengthy check-in process, we were finally shown to our rooms. One room was for us, while the other was for my sister and a friend. All I could think about was a refreshing shower and some much-needed rest."

"The following morning, over tea, my fingers nervously traced the rim of my cup. Should I tell him everything or hold back? The words felt heavy on my tongue, and I took a deep breath, glancing away for a moment before meeting his eyes again. "I…I don't know if I should say more," I murmured, I voiced my discontent with the events of the wedding day."

"Arif, your dad's behavior bothered me," I said, sipping my tea.

Arif looked genuinely apologetic. "I'm sorry about that. He can be…a bit much."

"A bit much? He nearly made a scene with the champagne!"

"Despite being married, it didn't quite feel real. I had envisioned a different reaction from Arif when I voiced my concerns, expecting him to understand and support me wholeheartedly. Instead, there was a nagging sense of disbelief and disappointment. How could he be so dismissive? I had imagined him taking my side, acknowledging the hurt his father's behavior had caused me. Instead, his apology felt almost perfunctory, like he was downplaying my emotions. It was as if my feelings were just an inconvenience to be smoothed over. The stark contrast between my expectations and reality left me feeling more isolated than ever. But what did I even want him to do? For that matter, how did I expect Arif to react? I didn't know it myself, but I craved something more, a genuine connection, a deeper understanding."

"Upon returning home after two days, the house felt empty without the presence of our relatives and friends who had already departed. Traditionally, there were more ceremonies and events we were supposed to partake in, but we never got around to completing them."

"To make matters worse, Arif fell ill with a high fever, followed by several members of my family and relatives. Even my brother and a few others had to be admitted to the hospital. My mother's focus shifted from me to him and part of me counted it as a blessing. No more bombardments of guilt trip through her eyes, I thought. The sudden wave of sickness among our loved ones left me questioning if it was some sort of punishment. The sudden wave of sickness among our loved ones left me feeling cursed. With everyone around me falling ill, it felt like we were trapped in a bad dream."

"How is he now?" I asked my mother, peering into my brother's room.

"Still feverish," she replied, a deep worry etched on her face. "I'm trying to keep him comfortable, but it's been tough."

I nodded, feeling helpless. "Is there anything I can do to help?"

She shook her head. "Just take care of yourself. We don't need more people falling sick."

I returned to my room, where Arif was sitting quietly, flipping through his phone. "This feels like a nightmare," I said, sitting next to him.

He looked up, concern in his eyes. "I know. It's like everything went wrong all at once."

"It's hard to believe this is how our married life is starting," I said, a lump forming in my throat. "I can't shake the feeling that the universe is conspiring against us."

Arif put his arm around me. "We'll get through this. Sometimes life throws us challenges to test our resilience. We just need to stay strong and hope for better days ahead."

I sighed, leaning into him. "You're right. I just wish things were different. It's so quiet and somber now."

"We'll get back to those happy times," he reassured me. "Let's just take it one day at a time."

I nodded, trying to believe his words. "Okay. One day at a time."

Thirty-Six

Arif's return to Maldives

"Can we order something to eat? I am hungry now,". Sid held his stomach and said.

"Of course, I would go with Tandoori fries, I know this cafe has the best ones".. Shifora declared. "Alright, will make it two" Sid added. After placing the order, Sid looked at Shifora, and asked, "Did Arif settle in Goa after marriage?".

Sid with his gaze intent. "What happened next?" he asked, his voice calm but urging her to continue.

"Despite our attempts to stay positive, I felt a sense of dread, as if this was just the beginning of a series of tests from the universe. All I could do was hope for the storm to pass and for our home to be filled with laughter once again."

Sid, noticing the tension in Shifora's expression, leaned in with genuine concern. "Why do you think it all happened?" he asked gently.

Shifora sighed, her eyes reflecting her inner turmoil. "I'm

not very sure," she admitted. "I was okay, though. Except for me, everyone else fell ill. It felt like some bizarre twist of fate."

Sid frowned thoughtfully. "It seems so unfair, all of it happening right after your wedding. But maybe it was just a series of unfortunate coincidences, not some cosmic punishment."

Shifora nodded slowly, appreciating Sid's attempt to rationalize the chaos. "Perhaps," she said softly, "but it didn't make it any easier to handle."

"After the wedding, during the time in Goa, he was still recovering from his illness, so our grand plans for sightseeing and visiting relatives turned into a marathon of binge-watching TV shows and sipping homemade soup. He had promised to help me find a job and even suggested that I might return to the Maldives soon. Arif stayed with us for about two weeks before he had to return to work. I could not join him as I had no place to live on the same island as he lived for his work. I Could not go to his home either in his absence. Of course, I had to work too, I didn't want to go to his home and stay there. There were no job opportunities on his home island."

"However, once he left, I found myself sitting at home, jobless and financially strained after the extravagant wedding that I didn't even enjoy."

"Who knew being a newlywed would be so… uneventful?" I mused one afternoon, scrolling through job listings for the hundredth time. Without a job, our family's financial situation became increasingly stressful. I was responsible for taking care of my parents, siblings, and myself, and I began to feel the weight of that responsibility like never before. I spent my days desperately chasing job opportunities, following up on applications I had submitted months earlier. Meanwhile, the pressure of staying at home while my husband was away only added to my stress.

"In our community, it's customary for the daughter to move in with her husband after marriage. So, neighbors and distant relatives began their investigative series, "Why Is Shifora Still at Home?" One of them even had the nerve to suggest that I go and meet the local MLA, practically begging for a job. This is common in the countryside. Every trip to the local market turned into an episode of 20 Questions."

"Why aren't you with your husband?" they'd ask. "Shouldn't you be working by now?"

"I wanted to scream, "If I had a rupee for every time someone asked me that, I wouldn't need a job!" But instead, ecstatically, I mumbled something vague about job hunting."

"This constant scrutiny led to arguments between my mother and me. She, too, was feeling the strain. "Why haven't you found a job yet, Shifora? You have so many qualifications!" she'd say, frustration seeping into her voice."

"My mother, never one to miss an opportunity, seized on this moment to voice her long-held skepticism about my education. "See, what's the use of all your degrees? Your cousins, who are less qualified, are earning much better than you. Yet here you are, sitting idle at home."

"Her words stung, adding another layer to my already mounting frustration. It felt like my entire life's efforts were being questioned and invalidated."

"As the days went by without any job prospects, I found myself in a dire financial situation. I had to borrow money from Arif to pay bills, something I had never wanted to do. This added to my feelings of inadequacy and failure. I felt like a contestant on a never-ending game show called "How Low

Can You Go?" and I was winning all the wrong prizes."

"Slowly, I began to feel the toll on my mental and emotional well-being. The constant worry about finances was like a persistent cloud hanging over my thoughts, casting a shadow of uncertainty. Bills piled up, and each day brought new anxieties about making ends meet. The pressure to find a job grew heavier with every rejection email and unsuccessful interview. It felt like I was constantly on edge, my confidence waning with each passing day of unemployment."

"The stress weighed heavily on my shoulders, leading to moments of exhaustion and an inability to focus on even simple tasks. It felt like I was carrying the weight of the world on my shoulders, and each day brought a new struggle to maintain a sense of hope and determination."

"How did my life become an endless loop of stress and anxiety?" I wondered aloud one evening.

Sid, lounging in his chair, raised an eyebrow. "Carousel, huh? Well, at least you get the occasional break for popcorn," he smirked before leaning in, his voice softening. "But seriously, Shifora, you've been through the wringer. What's your secret? How did you not just throw in the towel and start collecting cats?"

Shifora sighed, a small, wistful smile appearing on her face. "Honestly, Sid, there were days when hope seemed like a distant dream. But I guess it was the thought of a better future, the belief that things had to get better eventually, that kept me going. Plus, I couldn't let my family down. They were depending on me."

Sid leaned back with a knowing smile. "You know, Shif, I can only imagine how tough those critique sessions must have been. Your mom has a knack for digging deep, doesn't she?

But honestly, how did you handle it all? It must have taken a lot of strength to navigate that.

Shifora's smile faded a bit as she remembered those difficult conversations. "It was really hard, Sid. My mother never supported my education, and she used every opportunity to voice that. Those words cut deep, especially because I was already feeling like a failure."

Sid shook his head in disbelief. "That must have been incredibly painful. Did you ever confront her about it?"

Shifora nodded slowly. "Yes, I did. I tried to explain that I was doing my best and that finding a job wasn't as easy as it seemed. But it often felt like she wasn't listening. She was frustrated too, and in her way, she was just as stressed as I was. But those arguments took a toll on our relationship."

Sid reached out and gently touched her hand. "I'm sorry you had to go through all that, Shifora. But it sounds like you never gave up, despite everything."

Shifora squeezed his hand gratefully. "Thanks, Sid. I couldn't afford to. I had to keep pushing forward, for my family's sake and my own. It was the only way I could see to eventually find some peace and stability."

Sid exultant. "You're stronger than you realize, Shifora. And **sometimes, just surviving is a huge accomplishment.** Despite everything, I held onto a glimmer of hope. Maybe, just maybe, things would start looking up soon. After all, life had a funny way of surprising you when you least expected it.'

Thirty-Seven

Kala pani ki saza (punishment at dark sea)

"**Y**ou remember the one lady who supported our relationship back when we were in the Maldives?" Shifora questioned Sid.

Sid furrowed his brow, deep in thought. "Oh, Palomi! The one who kept asking you when you guys were getting married?"

"Yes, exactly!" Shifora nodded eagerly. "Well, one day, she called me with an unexpected opportunity. She was being transferred to the Andaman and Nicobar Islands for a pilot project with Taj Hotels and needed someone to join her team as a duty manager. The salary offered was way less than what I earned in the Maldives, but it was a significant shift in my career."

Sid leaned in, intrigued. "Did you take up the offer?"

"I discussed this with Arif, knowing it would mean living

apart again. However, after being unemployed and feeling the pressure to support myself and my family, I felt compelled to accept the job offer. You know Sid, I've always been independent and didn't like relying on others for financial support. I've been paying my bills since I was 14, so I was determined to take control of my situation." Shifora replied.

Sid nodded, encouraging Shifora to continue.

"Arif understood my decision, but my mother was less thrilled. She thought I should be with my husband, not off working in some remote islands. We had our discussions, and the plan was for me to work in the Andamans until I found a better job that would allow me to return to Arif.

"Unfortunately, finding a job in Maldives wasn't as easy as I'd hoped, and Arif's efforts to secure a job for me also were falling flat. To add to the complications, I was told that to get a dependent visa to join Arif in the Maldives, I'd have to change my name to an Islamic one and recite verses from their Holy book. I wasn't keen on changing my identity just for a visa. Returning to the Maldives became even more challenging."

"I collected all my strength and informed my mother about my decision to join the work in Andamans.

"My mother's face hardened, her tone sharper than ever. "Shifora, I don't know what has gotten into you since you got married. Running off to the Andamans while your husband is alone in the Maldives what kind of wife does that?" Her voice crackled with frustration. "People will talk! You think that doesn't matter?"

"My patience wore thin, but I kept my voice measured, trying to mask the ache of my mother's words. "Mama, Arif, and I have already discussed this. We both agreed I'd take this job. It's a good opportunity for me, and it's not like I'm disappearing. He supports my choice."

"My mother scoffed, her eyes narrowing. "Opportunity? Do you think an 'opportunity' is more important than being there for your husband? And tell me, Shifora, what will you do if you get pregnant over there? Just keep running around with your career?"

"A suffocated feeling clawed at my chest. "Mama, please, having children isn't the only purpose of marriage," I replied, my voice straining. "There's more to my life than that, can't you see?"

"But my mother cut me off, her voice rising with anger. "That's exactly your problem, Shifora! You think you're above what's expected. A woman's place is with her family, supporting her husband, preparing for children not chasing dreams on an island, away from everything she's supposed to be doing!"

"I clenched my fists, trying to keep my voice steady but feeling the sting of every word. "Why is it so hard to understand, Mama? Arif and I can handle this. He believes in my career, even if you don't."

"My mother's voice shook with fury. "That's because Arif has no idea what he's getting himself into! What are you even proving, running off on your own? You want independence, but when reality hits, you'll see how foolish all of this is. When you need your husband and he's not there, remember who told you so."

"My voice broke as I forced myself to speak. "Maybe I am being foolish, Mama. Maybe it's not the life you envisioned for me, but it's mine. Why can't you trust that I know what I'm doing?"

"My mother's eyes flared with hurt and anger, and she shot

back, "Because I know better than you, Shifora. You'll regret this. Mark my words."

I looked down, swallowing the bitterness, my voice barely a whisper. "We'll see."

"So, let me see if I get this," Sid said. "Your mom truly believed that a woman's life only begins and ends with marriage and family." He paused, giving her an understanding smile. "But you had dreams beyond that, Shifora. And it sounds like that alone was a bold step. How did it go from there?"

"Those days were a real challenge; staying at home felt like being stuck in a never-ending loop of expectations and traditional norms. I kept following up on my tickets to Andamans with Palomi, as I wanted to get out of the house asap."

"Flying into Port Blair in 2017 felt like stepping back in time. The city was clean, but there were mobile network issues, only BSNL worked, and I was using IDEA Sim. I managed to connect with my family through the hotel reception desk and update them on my whereabouts.

"The next day, I boarded a Makruzz ferry from Port Blair to Havelock Island. It was an early morning cruise that took about 2.5 hours. As I landed, I saw crowds of North Indian tourists flocking to the island. Manoj, our chauffeur, was waiting for me with a placard bearing my name. After introductions, we got into a luxury-looking (luxury to that surrounding) gray Innova. Swaraj Dweep, formerly known as Havelock Island, welcomed me with its serene beaches lined with towering coconut trees swaying gently in the breeze. The island's crystal-clear waters, teeming with colorful coral reefs and vibrant marine life, beckoned adventurers and nature lovers alike. It was a stark contrast to the bustling mainland, offering a tranquil escape despite its challenges."

"There was only one place in Havelock that baked good cakes back then, so we had to drive to the other side, collect the cake from Fat Martin (yes, that's the name of the restaurant), drive back to the main market, and then head to Radhanagar. It was quite the journey. "

"When we finally arrived at the resort, I was shocked to see the skeletal villas, it was a pre-opening resort, but I had expected something to be ready. I found myself in a place where I couldn't go back, couldn't change my decision, and was financially broke, a truly pathetic situation. The island was still living in the stone age, in a sense. It reminded me of Malgudi Days. Only the BSNL network worked, and bad weather often disrupted the network for days. We went days without talking to our families, resorting to handwritten letters to keep them updated. The limited transportation options and poor road conditions added to the challenges."

Sid grinned, thoroughly entertained. "Sounds like quite the adventure! How did you manage?"

"We got to know each other better, identifying our strengths and weaknesses along the way. Surprisingly, we unearthed hidden talents amidst the chaos. Evenings were often filled with our brand of humor, impromptu singing sessions, and the occasional antakshari, still one of my favorite pastimes to this day. It was like a flashback to my NCC camp days, where camaraderie was forged over simple joys. We played volleyball on the beach, canoed through crystal-clear waters, and embarked on nature walks that revealed the island's serene beauty. Amidst all this, we diligently handled resort operations, learning to juggle responsibilities while fostering a tight-knit team spirit."

Sid nodded thoughtfully. It sounds like you've learned a lot about facing challenges head-on and not giving up."

"Definitely," Shifora replied, reflecting on those days. "It was a period of growth in more ways than one."

Thirty-Eight

Distances getting Distant

"Andaman was an administratively protected area, I heard?" Sid Questioned.

"Yes". Shifora nodded her head.

"The Andamans, notorious for their capricious weather and sketchy cell service, greeted me with open arms and relentless cyclones. Trying to keep Arif and my folks back in Goa updated was like a game of hide-and-seek with telecommunication services, mostly hidden. Picture this, a pre-opening resort where we slogged just to pass inspections. Many bailed, but us out-of-towners? We held on for dear life, phone network permitting."

"Buying a local BSNL SIM was like adopting a moody pet, it worked when it felt like it. And my poor phone? Dived into the Andaman Sea quicker than I could say "hello, signal! It had become a ritual, and all those who landed there suffered a loss of their phones. I was no exception. My phone broke too.

So, I relied on borrowed phones from colleagues to give my folks a heads-up till I could get my new phone - for at least 3 months. Havelock, bless its heart, boasted a central market with the essentials, one grocery shop (Highland, where snacks were king), a unisex salon (a godsend for saltwater-ravaged hair), and restaurants with Wi-Fi more mythical than the Yeti. Need electronics? A pilgrimage to Port Blair was in order."

"Surviving the 2004 tsunami had turned the islanders into masters of minimalism. Humble, optimistic traits I tried to adopt as I grappled with phoneless existence for three months. Remember how Arif and I used to chat endlessly? Yeah, those became as rare as hen's teeth. Weekly check-ins replaced daily heart-to-hearts and emotional support? More like "Good luck with that." We drifted apart faster than a boat in a monsoon."

"I nagged Arif to spring me from this island purgatory, but no dice. understandings replaced misunderstanding, emotional support turned into an emotional tug-of-war, and "missing you" morphed into "don't call me." We were continents apart emotionally, Arif lounging on Maldives' beaches while I braved Andaman's tempests. Nothing was going as planned. Frustration brewed, I felt like my dreams were washing out with every cyclone."

"Arif did foot the bill for a while, but pride and a tight budget kicked in. My sister was in school, parents needed care, so I scrapped weekend bashes for budget-friendly hangouts with understanding pals. Work felt like a never-ending punishment, juggling tasks way beyond my job description just to get the resort up and running. I delved into Veer Savarkar's stories for solace, relating my plight to his 'Kala Pani' days a bit dramatic, but yeah, it got me through." So, Sid……" Shifora signed over a cup of coffee, "that's how I spent two years in 'island exile."

Sid giggled, stirring his coffee thoughtfully. "Well, it sounds like a tropical adventure of its kind. Lady Savarkar in 2019".

"Adventure, punishment, potato, potatoh," Shifora shrugged, a smile tugging her lips. "But yeah, I survived to tell the tale."

Return To Maldives

"**S**hhhhhhhhh... phshshhhhhhh..." The screech of wheels skidding across the tarmac cut through the quiet, followed by the low rumble of engines winding down.

Sid tilted his head toward the Island opposite the cafe, eyebrows raised. "Well, that's convenient. The airport's practically next door, isn't it? Was that an Emirates flight just now?"

Shifora smirked, not missing a beat. "Yep, Emirates... bringing in passengers and overpriced duty-free chocolates forever."

Sid grinned, shaking his head. "Speaking of landing, that brings me to my next burning question. How exactly did you manage to land *here* after your little Andaman adventure?"

Shifora continued, "As the economic pressure Kept growing, I urged Arif to find the job for me ASAP, at least bring me to where he was and I would do any kind of a job, as long as it helps me sustain my family's needs. Despite his efforts, at that time prevailing political issues between the countries posed obstacles.

"After spending two years in kala pani (black waters), I could not take it anymore. I reached out to my old friends who were already working in Maldives, and although I was not in touch with them ever since being in relation with Arif. They helped me secure a job in Maldives, the job that I am currently working. Without any hesitation, I accepted the job, and I was determined to make the most out of this opportunity. My mother was happy."

"Arriving in the Maldives on May 30th, 2019, my only objective was to recover what I had lost and return home for good. I had no interest in making friends or building relationships whatsoever. I knew what I wanted this time and was strong-minded not to divert from it. I just wanted to get back to my hometown as soon as I finished one year. I wanted to get secured and settle in Goa, my hometown for good. That was the plan."

"Arif was there at the airport to receive me. This was my first visit after marriage. There were no ceremonies, no rituals, and no celebrations in the Maldives by in-laws I Mean, for our marriage. Of course, it was two years old by now, but I think every married woman expects this. At least in India. Arif helped me settle in. He knew that I was in bad shape in every possible manner those days. I am grateful that he stood by me then, even though we were far away emotionally."

"My new workplace was warm, happy, and friendly. I met my new bosses and new colleagues. By now, all those situations and experiences for over 2 years have molded me into a different person. I had become rigid and not very open to anyone in terms of making new friends. I was not even approachable to my colleagues at work, I often spoke to them rudely. They tried their best to make me part of their groups, but I had some kind of aggression in me. I even heard that I was named "Sanki." Honestly, I couldn't explain the kind of anger I had within me. I was yelling and minding every small matter. I thought I was a bad person, and that I had done bad things in life. I was rejecting myself, and that also meant that I was behaving like that with Arif too. "Don't be around me, don't come near me." Literally, this was the feeling, and I guess unknowingly, I kept saying this to myself. My heart weighed heavy with an unshakable sense of unease. Professionally, I was performing admirably. My boss commended my skills and work ethic regularly."

"After work, I often went to my room and closed myself there. I was afraid of meeting new people and making new friends for many reasons. I didn't let my parents realize what I was going through. Of course, my mother could feel something was off, but I changed the topics and often displayed that I was very happy. I was trying my best to hide the turmoil in my heart, but…….. So, I started writing it down in my poems. When I uploaded these poems, my mother could feel there was something not right. I used to cry over tiny matters. I had become so insensitive to others but sensitive to myself."

"Oh wait, where was Arif then?" Sid interrupted.

"Arif worked in the same place as before, the resort 1 hour away from the Malé City. Hence he lived in the resort. I worked in a different organization now, hence I was living in Malé. Our weekly meetings, once filled with love and understanding, had turned into battlegrounds of arguments and resentment. The tender affection we once shared seemed like a distant memory, replaced by icy silence and wounded pride. Every time we argued, he kept counting the favors he did for me, specifically, "I entered the church for you, I got married to you even if my parents were against it." I had heard this sentence enough times by now in every argument of ours. He did not like it when I posted something on Facebook. He said, "If anyone from my relatives finds out it's you, my wife, what will they think about it?" Also, slowly, there were questions raised about my dress.

"Why was there so much aggression within you?" Sid question

"I didn't realize it at the time," Shifora replied softly. "It's hard to express the depth of turmoil one can feel inside".

Forty

Covid -19

❧❦❧

Thud.!!!!
'The sound echoed through the café, startling Shifora from her thoughts.
Something had fallen from the counter, caught in the playful sway of the breeze that seemed to be modeled through the open windows. Shifora immediately moved to help the staff gather the fallen objects, her movements swift and automatic. As she bent down, her eyes caught a small calendar among the scattered items, its pages displaying the stark instructions of COVID-19 safety rules.'

She picked up the calendar, her fingers tracing the edges as she stared at it, lost in a flood of memories. "Ma'am, may I have it?" The polite nudge from the café staff brought her back to reality. Shifora blinked, handing over the calendar with an absent smile.

Sid, who had been engrossed in helping as well, turned to

her with a curious look. " How can we forget that? Where were you during Covid times?" he asked, his voice gentle.

"Beginning of 2020, I had just returned to work from my Christmas break. I was dealing with my problems while the world had its own. People wanted to go places and I wanted to be home. Both of us were bound to make home wherever we were. A lockdown was announced from March onwards in the Maldives. No one knew what would happen next, including me. Once again, my plan of returning to Goa in a year was interrupted. I insisted on going back to India, but I stayed back, feeling as if my purpose in returning to the Maldives had still not been accomplished. No matter what, unless I achieved that, I was not going to leave. So, there I was, living in the Maldives with no salary for those four months. Arif was overlooking remotely, even though we did not meet once during that period. Slowly, things resumed, and we were kind of getting back on track."

"For the next year, there were on-and-off lockdowns declared in the country, and we worked from home for many months. That one-year plan of mine had now stretched into two years. It felt like trudging through quicksand, each day sinking me deeper into the mundane. My mornings began with a hollow routine, the alarm clock's blaring beep, a mechanically prepared cup of coffee, and the monotonous click of my laptop keys. Time seemed to mock me, stretching each day into an eternity. I would often find myself staring blankly at my screen, the cursor blinking back at me as if taunting my lack of progress."

"Weekends provided no respite. Instead of leisure, they were filled with a growing sense of frustration. I spent countless hours pacing my small apartment, my mind racing with thoughts of unfulfilled dreams and the stagnant life I felt trapped in. The walls of my room seemed to close in on me, each shadow and crack a reminder of my ambitions fading away."

"Every phone call with Arif was a painful reminder of the distance not just in miles, but in purpose. It had been almost over a year since Arif and I had met. Since every meeting of ours was taking a bad shape, Arif stopped coming to Malé to meet me. Each conversation seemed to follow a similar, frustrating pattern. One evening, as I dialed his number, I hoped for a breakthrough. The phone rang and Arif answered, his voice distant."

Forty-One

Attempt to Bridge the gap

"How was your day?" I asked, trying to keep my tone light.

"It was fine," he replied tersely.

Taking a deep breath, I decided to broach the topic that had been gnawing at me. "Arif, we need to talk about our plans. You promised we would start looking for a house, and it's been over a year now. We need to think about our future.

There was a heavy sigh on the other end. "Shifora, I can't handle this right now. The stress at work is too much, and I don't need you adding to it."

"My grip tightened on the phone, frustration bubbling up. "But Arif, you also said you'd work on getting a better job, maybe go back to school. We can't keep living like this, with no progress."

"Arif's voice grew sharp, a rare but telling change in his demeanor. "I told you, I don't want to study further. I just want a simple life, diving, fishing, living day by day. Why can't you understand that?"

"My shoulders slumped as I fought back tears. "Because that's not enough for me, Arif. I have dreams and ambitions. I can't just sit here and wait for things to happen."

"He was silent for a moment, then spoke softly but firmly. "Shifora, I'm not going to change. If you can't accept that, maybe we need to rethink everything."

"These words were conspiring, a cold confirmation of what I had feared. I closed my eyes, feeling the weight of our disconnect pressing down on me. "Maybe you're right," I whispered, with a barely audible voice."

"Our call ended with a hollow sense of finality, leaving me staring at my phone, the silence of the apartment amplifying my sense of isolation. I felt like I was losing him, not just to the physical distance, but to a chasm of unmet expectations and unfulfilled promises."

"Today we turn to one person to provide what an entire village once did, a sense of grounding, meaning, and continuity. At the same time, we expect our committed relationships to be romantic as well as emotionally and sexually fulfilling. Is it any wonder that so many relationships crumble under the weight of it all?"

"Oh wait, that sounds familiar" - Sid Interrupted, is that a quote from Ester Perell?

"Yes," Shifora nodded. "Marriage isn't just about finding someone to live with, it's about finding someone who shares your vision and values for the future. When ambitions diverge, it's not just about compromise, but understanding whether those dreams align enough to build a shared path forward."

"He didn't worry about the future, neither was he worried

about a safe house or securing a better life to start a family so that our children would not be burdened. Here it is, I had the answer. It was time for me to decide. Whereas I had ambitions, I still have for that matter. I wanted a high-paying job, secure many things, have something of my own, and become an entrepreneur. After all, how long will I work for someone else, I could equally work for myself. I kept overthinking."

"It was June 2021, and I felt severely ill, so much so that I was admitted to the famous ADK Hospital in Malé. Everyone in the office thought I had COVID. I am grateful for those four angels who were with me during those days. But it was not COVID. Doctors said my blood platelets had immensely dropped. This was the time I got questioned by many. "Where is your husband?" "Is everything okay between the two of you?" I said yes and assured them that he would come by morning. Those days Arif had not stepped out of the Island giving a reason that due to COVID waves they were not allowed to go out of the Island."

"I remember that day. I called up Arif and told him about the situation. I begged him, "Please come." He came to the hospital early in the morning at 5. I was relieved with his assurance, and Arif stayed with me for a week until I was better."

"It was July 1st of that year when Arif and I sat together and discussed our relationship. We realized that we had drifted too far apart. There was no way to come back. I had a different purpose, and my ambitions were crystal clear. I envisioned a future where I could build a loving family, provide a better life for my children, and ensure their future security. To achieve this, my first step was securing a stable home, a place where we could all feel safe and thrive. To realize this dream, I knew

I needed a high-paying job that could sustain our needs and aspirations. However, to attain such a job, I understood the importance of furthering my education. Education would pave the way for career advancement, financial stability, and ultimately, the ability to give my children the opportunities and security they deserved. In our conversation, we did not see our future together anymore. We had become different. It was like ripping apart the seams of something we once held so close, knowing full well that no amount of stitching could ever make it whole again. The love we shared had turned into a hollow echo, and no matter how much it hurt, we both knew the silence that followed was inevitable. Therefore, we mutually decided to part ways."

There was silence, Sid unaware of what to say, but still wanted to know what happened after.

Sid felt like hugging Shifora to assure her that he was there to comfort her, but didn't want Shifora to think that he was using the opportunity. He shifted in his seat, his wonder battling with the nervousness that tinged his voice. "So,…………… um, Sh….Shifora," he began hesitantly, "what happened next? I mean, after you and Arif decided to part ways?"

Forty-Two

Dealing with separation

"Oh no, this door is jammed again? How many times have I told you to grease it well!" 'The cafe supervisor's voice boomed across the room as he stormed in, completely oblivious to Shifora and Sid, the only customers tucked away in a quiet corner, to bring their attention to this yelling.'

Shifora turned to Sid with a quizzical look. "Ever felt like that jammed door, Sid?" The question slipped from her thoughts, borne of nosiness and a touch of whimsy.

Before Shifora could ponder her question, Sid interjected with a knowing smile, "I know exactly how it feels, like a jammed door." His response surprised Shifora. "How did he even guess what I was going to ask?" she wondered aloud, half amused and half intrigued.

There was a pause as Sid wrestled with his thoughts. He cleared his throat nervously before continuing, his voice tentative yet earnest. "So," he began, his words measured, "after you and Arif… talked about separating…………

"After talking about the separation, Arif decided to go back to the island (resort) where he lived. It started raining as if the universe was waiting for us to make this decision. Arif decided to return to his island right then, in the rain. As I walked him to the main gate, I realized that got soaked in the rain, weeping all the way, making sure no one would realize he was purposefully soaking himself in the downpour.

After what felt like an eternity, my phone rang. I answered, my voice trembling. "Arif?"

His voice was choked with emotion. "Shifora, I just reached the resort."

Are you okay?" I asked though I knew the answer.

"I'm sorry," he began, his voice cracking. "I'm sorry for not being the husband you deserved. I tried, but I just couldn't…"

I could hear the rain still falling on his end, a soft backdrop to his words. "Arif, it's not just you. We both tried, but sometimes love isn't enough," I replied, my tears mixing with the words.

"Remember when we first met? We had so many dreams, so much hope," he said, his voice distant as if he was lost in memory.

"Yes, we did," I whispered, but the words felt empty, like a reflex. I wanted to believe them. I wanted to hold on. But the truth was… I didn't have the strength. I didn't know how to let go, yet I didn't know how to keep us together. I was trapped between needing him and knowing I couldn't heal with him. He was my disease, and somehow, the cure too."

"But I failed you," he continued, the pain evident in his voice. "I couldn't give you the life you wanted, the stability you needed."

"It's not about failure, Arif. It's about growth and change," I tried to console him, though I was breaking inside. "We've both changed. Our dreams, our goals… they no longer align."

"I'll always care for you, Shifora," Arif said, his voice softening. "But you're right. It's time to let go."

"Goodbye, Arif," I said, my heart heavy with the finality of the word.

"Goodbye, Shifora," he replied, and with that, the call ended.

"On this side, I was sobbing too. When we fell in love, we celebrated our victories together, but now, as we separated, it felt like we were marooned on different islands alone and adrift. I had no friends, no family to lean on; just the heavy silence that wrapped around me like a suffocating blanket. The rain outside mirrored the storm within me, each drop a testament to the tears I shed, each rumble of thunder a reminder of the heartbreak I was enduring."

"Meanwhile, I could picture Arif out there, battling his demons, feeling the same void but perhaps in a different light. I could sense his despair, a silent echo of my own, yet it only deepened my loneliness. The weight of our shared memories pressed down on me, each joyful moment now a cruel reminder of what had slipped through our fingers. It was as if love had become a bittersweet ghost, haunting us both, leaving us to grapple with the wreckage alone."

"Little did I know, the choices we made that day would set off a chain of events neither of us could have foreseen, pulling us back into a world we thought we had left behind."

Forty-Three

Self Rejection

⸜⸝

"What's the best way to start your day? What thoughts would make it perfect for you?" Shifora leaned forward, clasping her hands together, elbows resting on the table between them, and enquired.

"Um… Well… I suppose… waking up knowing I can achieve whatever I set my mind to that day," Sid replied, scanning the table as if seeking answers amidst the clutter.

Shifora charmed, letting the silence hang,

"And why did you ask me that?" Sid relaxed back into his chair, leaning against the backrest.

"My day began with a single, relentless thought, to run away from everything, to escape, to erase myself… to die… to… to kill myself."

Sid sat up straight, his eyes widening even more as he exclaimed, "Oh no, no, no—not that!"

Shifora shifted uneasily, her fingers fidgeting with the edges of her sleeve. "Um, I'm not quite sure how to start this… It feels a bit strange talking about it now but looking back, I see how serious and misguided my thoughts were." Shifora sighed deeply, recalling the dark days.

"It was another lockdown period, and we had a mix of office work and working from home. Shifora continued, ironically, while the lockdown brought damage to the world, it forced me to reflect on myself, which only made me feel worse. "Why can't I find happiness? Why am I such a failure? What is my purpose?" These relentless thoughts gnawed at my soul and left me feeling hollow and desperate. Every minute, every second, I cursed myself, thinking, 'What have I done to myself? My mind had become a self-doubt. I forgot to clean my house, the once tidy space was now a cluttered mess. I forgot to cook, and when I did, I burnt the food. When I bought food, I forgot to eat it, leaving meals to spoil. The kitchen remained untidy and messy, a perfect reflection of my chaotic mind."

"Sometimes., I slept for two days straight, not feeling the need or energy to leave the bed. When I finally woke up, I felt more exhausted than ever. I hated the idea of going out, the very thought of facing the world filled me with dread. The noise outside was unbearable, and I loathed it when anyone wanted to visit. I avoided friends and family, coming up with excuses to keep them at bay. I had become absent-minded to the highest extent, forgetting important tasks and losing track of time. The simplest of chores felt insurmountable, and the isolation only deepened my sense of despair."

Sid raised an eyebrow, a blend of genuine concern and lightheartedness in his voice. "Two days straight? That's impressive, Shif. Sometimes the world can feel overwhelming, and it's perfectly okay to take a step back when you need to recharge. What do you think helped you through that time?"

"Yeah, it's hard to even think about facing the world when every sound just kicks up reminders of what's missing." Shifora continued.

"The aggression within me was growing. The sense of hopelessness was overwhelming. I sat in my room, staring at the walls that seemed to close in on me. I couldn't escape my mind. I felt trapped, suffocated by the weight of my expectations and failures. The thoughts of ending it all began to surface more frequently. It seemed like the only way to silence the torment within."

"I started to plan, thinking about how I could make it quick and painless. I wrote letters to my loved ones, apologizing for being such a burden. I thought about the impact my death would have on them, but even that wasn't enough to pull me back from the edge. I used to cry until my throat jammed and until I needed a bio break, which was generally after an hour. I would eat only morsels and then start crying again. The mantra was, eat, cry, repeat. I was filled with a heavy sense of isolation and self-loathing."

"I would wake up every morning with a weight on my chest, dreading the hours ahead. The thoughts that plagued my mind were relentless, a continuous loop of regret and self-blame. "Why did I make those decisions?" "How could I have been so selfish?" The more I pondered, the more I sank into a pit of despair."

Forty-Four

Self Harming

"Oh Gosh!!! Hope you did not harm yourself out of these overpowering emotions?" Sid quizzed naturally.

"I banged my head against the wall, hoping the pain would drown out the thoughts," Shifora confessed, her voice trembling. "I hit my hands hard on the ground until they bruised, feeling the physical pain as a temporary escape from the mental anguish. I choked my throat, desperate to end it all. I swallowed sleeping pills, but they didn't work. I felt like a failure even at ending my own life."

"Whaaaat?!!! Oh, wait!! How come the sleeping pills didn't work?" sid Interrupted

Shifora countered, "Apparently, those were my muscle-relaxing pills. I consumed them thinking that if I overtook them, it would help me settle the chaos in my mind".

Sid's eyebrows shot up in surprise. "Muscle relaxants?" he

repeated, "incredulous. Shifora, that's… I don't even know what to say."

Shifora looked down, and with a faint tone, she continued. "As soon as I opened my eyes late, that Sunday morning, an unexpected notification from Google Photos flashed on the cracked screen of my iPhone. I had been browsing aimlessly when a picture from years ago flashed on my screen, a vibrant snapshot of me smiling, surrounded by friends, full of life and joy. The photo, so full of brightness and hope, seemed to mock my present misery. It felt like a cruel reminder of how far I had fallen from that happy version of myself.

"The image burned into my mind, an unrelenting specter that refused to fade, intensifying the weight…. …weight of my guilt trip, as if my happiness had stabbed me, every laugh and smile now a painful contrast to the emptiness I felt. It was as if the universe was throwing my past happiness in my face, just when I was at my lowest. Every shred of positivity seemed to have evaporated from my world, leaving me engulfed in a suffocating fog of hopelessness. The sight of that cheerful photograph, the embodiment of everything I had lost, was the final, bitter nudge that drove me toward that desperate decision."

"It was an agonizing symphony of despair, regret, and self-loathing. The cacophony in my head was relentless. My mother's words echoed in my mind, not as comfort but as a painful reminder of her expectations and the pride she had in me that I felt I was failing to uphold. Her face, a blend of disappointment and worry, flashed before my eyes, and it felt like she was silently chastising me from beyond, pushing me further into the abyss."

"In a fit of rage and frustration, I stormed through my

apartment. I could feel the heat of my anger and sadness converging into a single, blinding force. I grabbed the bedsheet and, with a violent swipe, threw it across the ceiling fan. The action was almost mechanical, driven by a need to create some sense of order in the chaos that had engulfed my mind. My heart pounded in my chest as I pulled up a chair, and placed it beneath the fan. The room was spinning, and I could barely hear my thoughts over the din of my emotions."

"I kept replaying moments of failure and disappointment. The relentless feeling of being a burden, of never being enough, gnawed at me. I remembered failed projects, missed opportunities, and every word of criticism that had ever stung. Each memory felt like a knife twisting deeper into my psyche. The weight of all these emotions, the aggression, the deep sadness, the paralyzing fear of never finding peace, coalesced into a singular, desperate urge. I could see no end to the darkness that enveloped me, no light breaking through the thick, suffocating clouds of despair. It wasn't just about ending my life, it was about escaping an existence that felt unrelentingly cruel and hopeless."

"The silence in the room was deafening. The curtains were drawn, casting long shadows across the walls. I could hear the faint hum of life outside, but it felt like a world apart. I thought it was a chaotic storm, battering against the fragile walls of my mind. I was almost about to execute the plan to hang myself from the only fan in the room. For that last time, I stared at that one-line note which stuck on the mirror of my dressing table, that read - NO ONE IS RESPONSIBLE, IT'S MY DECISION."

"Just as I was about to step off the chair, my phone rang. It was afternoon by then, an unusual time for Waseem to call. He was a busy man, and we usually spoke in the evenings, if at all. The surprise of his video call in the afternoon jolted me out of my trance."

Forty-Five

The Saviour

"Oh, so you answered his calls and never tried to receive mine?" Sid asked, eyebrows furrowed in jealousy.

Shifora silently nodded "yes" and continued. Even though I had pushed away all my friends and relatives, avoiding their phone calls and messages, Waseem's call was unavoidable. He had always been like an elder brother to me, a constant pillar of support. Even when he was abroad, he made sure there was someone in his stead to be there for me whenever I needed it. His guidance, protection, and unwavering presence, even from afar, were things I couldn't easily disregard. Waseem had been my anchor, and his call was a lifeline I couldn't ignore, no matter how much I tried to shut the world out.

"The phone screamed for the second time, bringing me out of my thoughts of what Waseem meant to me. With trembling hands, I swiped the screen of the phone, Waseem's face appeared on the screen of a video call. I looked disheveled and exhausted, and I tried to compose myself. My unkempt hair and tired eyes told a story of neglect and inner turmoil."

"Hey, Shifora, I hope I'm not catching you at a bad time. You look……(Waseem is lost for words) ..well, you don't look like your usual self. Everything okay?" Waseem's voice coming through the screen felt like a soothing balm to my frazzled nerves.

(Her voice was flat, eyes distant.) "Yeah, whatever. What's up? (Shifora Attempted a weak smile, but her voice betrayed her exhaustion).

"This is not normal you Shifora, you seem so off, and your place looks… well, a bit cluttered. What's going on? You've been on my mind lately." Waseem sounded worried.

(Eyes welling up as I looked around my untidy space, Impatiently) *"Not really. Just… not in the mood for a chat right now."* Irritated Shifora threw her phone away in the bed, while the video call was still on, Waseem through the video call saw the fan with the bed sheet hanging.

Waseem reacted quickly, " Oh no no no no……..hey Shifora, look here, see who wants to talk to you?" right then Waseem's daughter and wife showed up on the screen. " see how much joy she brings? Sometimes, it's these little connections that remind us of the good."

I wiped my tears, took the phone in my hands again, and looked at the toddler. Looking at the toddler's face, I just continued sobbing… (I could not utter a word)

"Waseem's voice broke through the haze, laced with urgency. "You!!! … (pause…) Listen, we're here for you. It's okay to feel down. We all have those moments. But if you don't start talking to me soon, I might just have to come over there myself. And if that takes too long, I swear I'll call the police, a hospital, or even your family. I just need to know you're okay."

"I understand, Shifora. You don't have to go through this alone. We're just a call away." Waseem's wife ensured.

"Instead of feeling frightened at the thought of involving my family, a wave of warmth washed over me. At that moment, I realized Waseem wasn't just throwing around empty threats—he truly wanted me to be alive. He cared."

"Waseem, I… I don't know what to say," I sobbed, my voice breaking. "It just… it hurts so much. But hearing you say that… means I'm not alone. I… I need that right now."

"Shifora, listen to me," he said, his voice firm but gentle. "You're not a burden. I know it feels like everything is closing in, but I promise you, there's a way out. You're stronger than this moment. Don't let it win."

My chest was heavy with an unbearable flood of emotions. "But what if I can't find that strength? What if I'm just… too far gone?"

"Then let me help you find it. Please, don't shut me out. You're not alone in this. We'll figure it out together. I won't let you go without a fight."

A shiver ran through me. "Waseem, what if the fight is too hard? What if I don't want to fight anymore?"

"Then I'll fight for you. You're worth it, Shifora. You deserve to see tomorrow, to feel the sunlight again. Don't give up on that hope, no matter how dim it feels right now."

(*Breathing deeply, trying to steady my emotions*) "Thank you, Waseem". There was a Sob and just silence…..

The call ended leaving me to bring back to the current world.

"After talking to him that day, I felt a flicker of hope. The realization that someone cared, that there was still a connection to the world outside the pain, made me step back from the brink. I knew I had to hold on. Dubte ko tinker ka sahara (A drowning person clings to a straw.), Even if just for a little longer, I had to believe that things could get better. That day I had no words or rather I was not in a position to Thank Waseem enough, but as I was getting better, all I could do was write something for him, if not express it by saying. I think I could write a book about him one day just to thank him."

"Oh wow, you write too? That's amazing, Shifora," Sid said softly, his eyes full of admiration. "I guess I have even more reasons to thank Waseem now, don't I?"

After going through this suicidal reminiscence, Shifora breathed a deep sigh of relief, sipped some water, looked at Sid, and said "Yeah".

Forty-Six

A New Dawn

"How did you collect yourself from all of this?" Sid Invoked

"It wasn't easy again. I took it super slow because until I could stand with myself, no one else would. No matter how I put it all together, I had to take that first step" Shifora Admitted.

"After a call with Waseem that day, I slept again. But when I woke up the next morning, I noticed a flurry of missed calls from him. I texted back quickly, "I'm fine." His response was a simple emoji, a sigh of relief, that somehow made me smile. I felt an overwhelming need for assurance, a spark of faith from someone who believed in me to help reignite the flame of my life. That call from Waseem wasn't just a lifeline pulling me back from the edge, it was a strong reminder to trust in myself again. It rekindled the dreams I had tucked away and whispered the purpose of my life back to me, urging me to rise from the ashes of despair. In that moment, I realized I wasn't just surviving, I was being given a second chance to truly live."

"Waseem gifted me a few counseling sessions. At first, I was hesitant. Did I need help? But as I sat in that cozy office of a coach, sharing my story, I realized how essential it was to talk about my feelings. Each session peeled back layers I didn't even know existed, illuminating the positives in me."

"Gradually I started my routine, determined to reclaim my life. First things first, I cleared the mess in my room, tossing out empty milk cans, discarded bottles, and all the other remnants of my former life that had cluttered my space and mind. With each item I threw away, I felt a weight lift, as if I was shedding not just physical clutter but the emotional baggage that had held me captive."

"I dusted off my yoga mat, ready to restart my morning routine. As I moved through each pose, breathing deeply, I felt my body awakening, shaking off the remnants of despair. After yoga, I began my morning walks around Malé. The fresh air filled my lungs, and with every step, I felt more alive."

"Cautiously, I began making friends in Malé. I said yes to invitations for dinners and even joined a group for island hopping. Laughter and shared experiences filled my days, reminding me of the joy life could bring."

"I talked to my boss to request more work. Since one of my colleagues was heading on maternity leave, part of her responsibilities were shared with me. But that was still not enough for me. It was like 'overworking se darr nahi lagta sahab, pyar se darr lagta hai' (I am not afraid of work but of love)." The universe seemed to be conspiring in my favor, nudging me toward the light. I felt its presence in the kindness of new friends, the laughter shared over meals, and the quiet strength I found within myself. I was slowly reclaiming my life, piece by piece."

"As long as my mind was occupied, I could keep the darkness at bay. But the moment there was a space or a breather, all the guilt I carried came crashing back. The guilt of marrying someone against the community, even after so many red signals, treating my mother badly, and the feeling of spoiling Arif's life, being the reason for breaking his first marriage, was unbearable. The weight of it was crushing me, I wanted to hide my face inside the earth where no one could find me."

Sid raised an eyebrow, a smirk tugging at his lips. "Now I know why you avoided my calls and why you avoided meeting me?"

Shifora looked at Sid and her eyes answered "yes", and softly, shaking her head she said. "If only I could've booked a one-way ticket to oblivion. But no, it was more like an all-inclusive trip to Self-Criticism City."

"Ah! the classic dilemma. Sid Remarked.

Shifora nodded thoughtfully, her eyes reflecting a mixture of sadness and hope. "It's true," As Deepak Chopra mentions in *The Seven Spiritual Laws of Success*, 'In the process of letting go you will lose many things from the past, but you will find yourself.' Sometimes, losing ourselves is just the beginning of finding who we are." she said softly.

Forty-Seven

The New Life

❧

" What's the toughest part of this new routine?" Sid conceded.

"Well, let's just say my yoga poses are a work in progress. My 'downward dog' looks more like a confused puppy. And don't even get me started on 'tree pose', I'm more of a leaning sapling right now." Shifora Laughed.

"Ah, the classic yoga struggle. But it sounds like you're finding your balance literally and figuratively." Sid supported Shifora.

"I'm getting there. And spending time with friends? That's been a game-changer. I'd say I'm becoming a pro at socializing and pretending my life is more put together than it is." Shifora stated. "My days were a battlefield of trying to keep up appearances while battling my demons. Shifora continued.

This continued for some time. No one at the office or back home knew what was going on in my life. I approached and contacted many psychologists to bring me out of this. I wasn't able to get appointments at the local clinics here in Male', so I approached someone in Goa. I googled her profile, read her reviews, and contacted her through the number mentioned on her profile. Dr. Akshada Amonkar. Only after talking to her did I feel as if a weight was lifted. Maybe I was afraid that my friends and family would judge me if I spoke about what I felt. Why not? There were a couple of them who said to my face, 'It was your choice, don't drag us into this.' I accepted it was my mistake and my choice, so I had to bear the consequences. But there was one person who knew something was not right, Lancy sir.

He was one of those four angels who were by my side that day when I was in the hospital lying in bed with low platelets. Even though I wasn't open with anyone those days, he almost guessed it. Lancy sir worked as AVP IT at the same workplace as I did. He made me sit and questioned me, but I was stubborn as ever and didn't open my mouth. He asked me about my future, and I said I always wanted to study further. I would like to be a student again. I like studying. That is true. I like studying even now.

This plan went on for a month, but I hadn't taken admissions anywhere yet. Lancy sir kept nudging me now and then. He helped me get information from a couple of colleges I was interested in, called up his contacts, and found the information. Finally, I made a choice and enrolled in a distance MBA program at NMIMS Mumbai. I must say, I enjoyed the MBA journey. It was a two-year course. I think that was one of the good things that happened to me during COVID. The studies diverted my mind from the turmoil inside me. Apart from Waseem, an MBA saved me. Needless to say, my mother had her say in this too, she was against me studying any further.

Sid, now more relaxed, nodded with understanding. "It sounds like those studies were a lifeline for you. It's amazing how sometimes the most unexpected things can pull us out of the darkest places."

Shifora chuckled lightly, "Yeah, who knew an MBA could be more therapeutic than a psychologist, huh?"

Forty-Eight

Filing for Divorce

❧

'S id looked at Shifora with curious eyes. "Did you also file for legal divorce or was that it?"

Shifora took a deep breath, her brows furrowing slightly as her eyes fixed intently on the horizon. Her lips pressed together in a thin line, conveying a solemn resolve. She carried a weight in her expression, a seriousness that spoke of difficult decisions and heartfelt conversations to come.'

"That year when I went home in December for the Christmas holidays, I didn't want to start a new year with a heavy heart. So, I decided to open up to my parents about what had happened between Arif and me, and the decision we had made."

Sid interrupted, "Oh wait!! Your parents didn't know yet?"

Shifora nodded her head right to left in her answer.

She paused, recalling the anguish of that evening. "Seeing my father break down was devastating. He had always been my rock, the strongest man I knew. To witness him crumble under the weight of our family's pain shattered me. My sister and I knelt beside him, he was blaming himself for everything, crying like I had never seen him before, not even when we lost his mother. I remember holding his hand tightly, desperate to comfort him," Shifora recalled, her own eyes moistening with the memory. " 'Don't cry, daddy,' I whispered, 'everything will fall back into place. I'll make sure of it.' Dad's voice broke as he choked back tears, "All I wanted was to see you all happy, nothing else."

And my brother sat silently in the corner, his presence a quiet reassurance amidst the chaos. He could sense that something was amiss, though he didn't fully understand what was happening.

"My mother's tears flowed freely, her grief palpable as if we had lost a beloved family member. The weight of our collective pain hung heavy in the room."

"That night, we all felt as if a heavy burden had been lifted from us."

"The very next day, the inquiries for divorce began," Shifora continued, her voice steady now, despite the memories still raw. "I hired a lawyer to handle the legal formalities. It felt like writing a detailed memoir, how we met, how we fell in love, how we lived, and why we wanted to separate. Every detail dissected and documented."

"It took roughly a year," she emphasized, reflecting on the drawn-out process. "But that was just the beginning."

Turning to Sid, she explained, "When I approached the church to understand the formalities of nullifying our marriage, I was directed to the Bishop House in Panjim. The priest there was kind and helpful, guiding me through the intricate steps of annulment."

The next day, my sister and I drove to Panjim from Sanvordem. The car ride was filled with a heavy silence, broken only by the sound of the engine and the occasional honk.

"Are you sure about this, Shifora?" my sister asked, her eyes glancing at me with concern as she navigated the winding roads. "I mean, can't you and Arif think it over one more time?"

I sighed, staring out the window at the passing scenery. "We have thought about it, over and over again. The decision wasn't made lightly. We tried to make it work, but it just isn't right for either of us."

"But what exactly went wrong? You both seemed so in love," she pressed, her voice soft but insistent.

"It's not about love anymore," I explained, turning to face her. "It's about fundamental differences in our goals, our values, and what we want from life. We tried to bridge that gap, but it kept growing wider."

She nodded slowly, absorbing my words. "And you're ready for this process? They say it can take up to two years."

"I can't start a new year with this heavy heart. I need closure, and this is the only way to get it." I replied with a wry smile.

My sister reached over and squeezed my hand. "Alright. Let's do this. Together."

"We reached the Bishop House and enquired about the process of nullification of the marriage. They warned me it would be more than a two-year process," Shifora continued with a smirk, "and asked if I was ready for that. I had no choice but to say yes," she admitted, a touch of irony in her tone. "Again, it involved recounting our entire journey separately, mind you. How we met, how we fell in love, and ultimately, why we parted ways. They conducted thorough investigations to verify our statements," Shifora added, shaking her head slightly. "Six months for that. Then they gave us another six months to reconcile or reconsider. As if reliving the past wasn't enough, they wanted us to dwell on it some more.

She sighed, a mix of frustration and resignation evident. "After statements from witnesses and more waiting, we finally reached the judgment phase. It felt like a perpetual loop of reliving those moments exhausting mentally, to say the least."

Sid questioned Shifora, "So, is the marriage officially annulled?"

Shifora shook her head.

She questioned herself unofficially. When the answer did not come from within, she knew, she was still figuring out the missing jigsaw pieces of her own identity.

Forty-Nine

First Encounter with Self

"Wait... so you stayed back in the Maldives until *everything* was settled?" Sid asked, his voice low and filled with intrigue like he was piecing together a mystery. "How did you handle it?".

Shifora nodded slowly, her expression reflective. "Yes, I did. Those days were a cyclone of emotions. I remember feeling utterly terrible like my senses were on vacation without me. To top it off, my sister fell severely ill while staying with me. Can you believe it? I was so out of it that I couldn't properly care for her. That guilt of not being there for my sister just added to the weight I was already carrying. Maybe I didn't know how to handle my feelings amidst hers. Perhaps I wanted to heal just as much, even though her illness didn't manifest like others.

Shifora paused, a wry smile touching her lips as she continued, "I must have looked fine to everyone else, but inside, I was crumbling. Books became my refuge, my way of pretending everything was normal. Studying was my lifeline, even though deep down, I knew I was a walking emotional wreck."

Shifora sighed deeply, her thoughts drifting back to those desperate days. "I tried therapists, and psychiatrists all of them seemed fixated on my divorce. They handed out calming pills like they were handing out candy, but they didn't calm me down. I wanted someone who could guide me through this storm, someone I could trust implicitly. But I was paralyzed by fear, unsure who to confide in. I feared my vulnerability might be exploited, and my struggles used against me. It felt like navigating a maze blindfolded, hoping not to stumble into deeper darkness."

She paused, a flicker of frustration crossing her face. "I needed real help, not just someone ticking off boxes on a diagnosis form. I wanted reassurance and genuine compassion. Instead, I found myself questioning every word, every prescription. Trust became a luxury I couldn't afford, not when the stakes were so high and my heart so fragile."

Then Shifora brightened a bit, "But you know what shook me out of my funk? Hospital duty. Yeah, one of our colleagues landed in the hospital, and we had to take turns staying with her. That's when I met this wise, seasoned lady from our office, educated, compassionate, the whole package. We had worked together for a year by then but never really connected until then."

As she reminisced, a soft chuckle escaped Shifora, recalling their unexpected bond. "I've always been cautious about forging new relationships, especially friendships," she began. "But Mary, she saw right through my reservations. It was during one of those challenging weeks when our colleague fell seriously ill and was hospitalized for a week. Mary and I were buddies to take turns staying by her side during our off-office hours. Those long hours in the hospital ward became a space where Mary gently coaxed my story out of me."

She paused, reflecting on those transformative moments. "Listening to Mary share her struggles while caring for our colleague, put my pain into perspective. It was like she held up a mirror to my emotions, and suddenly, the weight I carried didn't seem so insurmountable. Her empathy and understanding were like a balm to my soul during that turbulent time."

Shifora's eyes softened with gratitude as she continued, "Mary helped me not only to reflect on myself but also to accept myself. She became my guardian angel, the only person I felt safe enough to open up to in years. And you know what she told me? "Shifora, it is easy to forgive others. The real victory and peace lie in forgiving oneself. But all it takes is little courage.

I had heard of forgiving others, saying sorry, all that jazz. But forgiving myself? That was a game changer." She recommended some books that became my lifeline during that period of healing. One of them, a book on motivation and self-discovery, resonated deeply with me. It was as if those pages were written just for me, guiding me through the process of reclaiming my strength and finding peace within myself. *Everything that's coming into your life you are attracting into your life. And it's attracted to you by the images you're holding in your mind. It's what you're thinking. Whatever is going on in your mind you are attracted to...........The Secret" by Rhonda Byrne."*

She leaned in, her voice earnest, "It felt like I finally found a container big enough to hold all the storms raging inside me. In the chaos of my self-destruction, I had missed the silver linings in my life, and wasted time complaining about things that didn't matter."

A naughty glim sparkled in her eyes, "And then, cue 'The Secret' by Rhonda Byrne. No, no, I'm not going to shove it down your throat, but let me tell you, that book found me at the perfect moment. You know how they say, 'When the student is ready, the teacher appears'? Well, 'The Secret' was my unexpected guru."

"If I had stumbled upon that book earlier, I probably would have rolled my eyes and dismissed it, she said. But after everything, it was exactly what I needed, a dose of positivity that I didn't know existed."

Sid gayed warmly. "It's amazing how the right people come into our lives at just the right time, isn't it?"

"And the right book too," Shifora replied. "Mary's friendship was a lifeline for me. She not only listened but also encouraged me to see beyond my pain."

Sid nodded thoughtfully. "It sounds like she gave you the perspective you needed to start forgiving yourself."

Shifora nodded in agreement. "Exactly, her guidance helped me to accept myself and my journey, flaws and all."

Fifty

The Journey begins

'Sid raised an eyebrow, sensing there was more to the story. "Is that why you have so many self-healing-related posts on social media? "

Shifora gladsome, "Well, I didn't have a guide or anything. While doing the MBA, one of the assignments in marketing was to create our profile on social media platforms. That included Instagram. Hence, I started the account mid 2022. Like everyone else, I used to scroll through the reels, and eventually like everyone else, I got addicted to it too. One day I randomly stumbled upon a 21-day self-love challenge.

"During those days, there was this self-love challenge on Instagram. I participated in it and religiously followed the assignments they gave. And let me tell you, some of them were pretty out there. One day, they asked us to walk in nature, and another day to complete a series of Surya namaskar. Other tasks included writing a letter to your younger self, meditating for ten minutes, cooking a healthy meal, and even dancing like no one was watching."

"One day, the assignment was to list five things you were grateful for. Another day involved creating a vision board of your dreams and aspirations. There was a task where we had to do something kind for a stranger and another where we had to spend an hour doing something we loved as a child. Some days we had to practice positive affirmations, spend time with a loved one without distractions, or take a digital detox for a few hours."

"Then came the day they asked us to write down everything we loved about ourselves. Imagine staring at a blank page for hours. It was like trying to find a needle in a haystack. Why was I unable to write anything about myself? The thought gnawed at me, revealing the depth of my self-doubt and the long road I had ahead in my journey toward self-love. It was then I realized how disconnected I was from my worth, my value. It was a wake-up call, and that self-love challenge became a pivotal part of my journey towards healing and self-discovery."

"I was filled with self-doubt, self-criticism, and perhaps a lack of self-esteem. It could have been telling me that I wasn't good enough, didn't deserve love or appreciation, or that there was nothing noteworthy about myself worth acknowledging. These inner voices often stem from past experiences, societal pressures, or personal insecurities that cloud one's ability to recognize and appreciate their own strengths and positive qualities."

Sid guffawed, "Sounds like a treasure hunt for your soul."

Shifora grinned, "Exactly! I reflected on the good moments, the things I was proud of, and the qualities that made me unique. It was like discovering a hidden treasure within myself."

"Simultaneously, One of the topics that *The Secret* addressed was self-love," Shifora began, her voice carrying a note of conviction. "I could feel this and agreed with what the author wanted to communicate through this topic. I realized that I had punished myself enough. It was time for forgiveness and moving on. Eventually, I understood that if I didn't love myself, how would I be able to accept someone else? No matter what, first you have to love yourself, and treat yourself the way you would want your loved one to treat you. Shifora took a deep breath, her eyes reflecting the positive changes she had undergone."

Sid signaled the staff for another coffee, then turned back to Shifora. "So, tell me, how did you even realize you needed self-healing? Was there a moment that clicked for you?"

Shifora took a deep breath, her fingers tracing the rim of her coffee cup. "It was actually through Instagram," she admitted with a small laugh. "One evening, I was scrolling mindlessly when a post caught my attention. It had this beautiful serene landscape and a list of symptoms that were all too familiar: constant exhaustion, unexplained sadness, losing interest in things I used to love, and just feeling empty inside."

Sid leaned in, intrigued. "Wow, social media is being useful for once. What did the post suggest you do?"

"It mentioned practicing mindfulness, seeking therapy, journaling emotions, and setting healthy boundaries," Shifora replied. "But what struck me was a video I watched by Gaur Gopal Das. In it, he talked about the importance of self-healing and how recognizing the need to heal is the first step. He said something like, 'Healing yourself is crucial because you cannot pour from an empty cup. You need to be whole and healthy to truly give to others and live a fulfilling life.' It was like a light bulb went off in my head."

Sid's eyes widened. "Gaur Gopal Das, huh? That guy knows how to touch the soul. So, what did you do after watching the video?"

"I downloaded a few meditation videos from "level supermind by Beer Biceps", started journaling my thoughts and feelings, and even reached out to a therapist online," Shifora replied. "Each suggestion felt like a lifeline. Mr. Das's words, along with that Instagram post, made me realize how badly I needed to heal."

"That's incredible," Sid said, his eyes reflecting genuine admiration. "So, social media wasn't just a time waster for you".

"Exactly," Shifora nodded.

So, Shifora, I remember you mentioning something about '7 shades of Self-Healing' in one of the stories on Instagram, suggesting it is like a self-help rainbow or something?" Sid's eagerness heightened.

"Ah, *'7 Shades of Healing'*! Yes, healing does come in many forms," Shifora replied with a smile. "I've focused on seven key shades, each inspired by the colors of the rainbow. Every shade brings out a new way to mend and rediscover yourself."

"Fascinating! So, it's like you've got a whole spectrum of self-repair techniques. I'm on the edge of my seat here, what's the first color in this healing rainbow?"

Fifty-One

The Healing Rainbow

'Shifora tilted her head, a teasing shimmer in her eye. "Since we're on the topic of rainbows, Sid, can you name all the colors?"

Sid's lips curled into a playful smirk. "Oh, that's a cinch. There's red, blue, green, and… uh, purple, right?"

Shifora raised an eyebrow, a teasing smile tugging at the corners of her mouth. "You are almost there. But I'm afraid you're missing a few shades."

Sid with feigning innocence. "Well, it looks like my color theory might need some self-healing to enlighten me?"

Shifora cackled. The same one, which Sid used to like about her in college days. Sid was overjoyed to finally witness this laughter.

Sid was blushing.

Shifora leaned closer, her eyes sparkling. "Let's just say there's a full spectrum involved, much like the journey of self-healing I've been talking about. Maybe I'll give you a private lesson on the rest of the colors later. Deal?"

Sid's eyes twinkled with intrigue. "Deal. And I'm guessing this lesson might come with a splash of your charm?"

Shifora's laughter was like a melodic chime. "Oh. But for now, let's look into the colors of healing and see where that leads me."

Shifora sighed, taking a sip of her coffee. "Well, I did a lot of study on myself. Like, brainstorming into the last seven years of my life."

Sid raised an eyebrow. "Oh wait - 7 years?"

"Yes, 7 years from the time I got Married in 2017, till I am Healed" Shifora replied.

"Ohhh!! Now I know Why it is 7 **shades of healing** everywhere - Sid's eyes sparkled.

Shifora looked at Sid and Smiled in agreement.

"Wow, that's next level, man! I can't even imagine how deep you have thought of all that!" He threw his hands up in surprise and continued. "But I'm really curious about this seven-year journey of self-exploration. You mentioned the seven shades, how do you relate them to the colors of the rainbow? I'm both amazed and a bit confused."

With excitement in her eyes, she replied, "The answer lies right in your question!"

Looking even more surprised, he asked, "Seriously? How so?"

Yes! I realized that each color of the rainbow represents a different element of personal development. I dedicated each color to a specific aspect of my self-exploration journey."

Thinking deeply, he responded, "That's fascinating. So, how did you incorporate these colors into your self-healing process? How did each one play a role in your journey?"

Fifty-Two

Red of Rainbow – Self-Reflection

"Sid, do you ever just… look back and cringe at some of the things you've done?" Shifora asked, a wry smile on her lips.

Sid grinned, "Oh, all the time. It's called being human. What's on your mind?"

Shifora groaned. "Honestly, it's been rough. I keep thinking about all the things I could've done differently. Like with Arif? We were such good friends, but there were times I just… shut him out. But there were moments when I felt off, and instead of talking to him, I kept everything bottled up. I was afraid of being vulnerable, I guess. I thought if I let him in on my struggles, he'd see me differently. But looking back, I realize how silly that was."

Shifora took a deep breath, her gaze fixed on the swirling foam of her repeat order of cappuccino. "It was after everything fell apart. The marriage, the constant struggle, and the overwhelming sense of being lost. I knew I needed to understand how I had gotten there in the first place."

Sid nodded, his eyes encouraging her to continue. "That must have been a lot to process. How did you start reflecting on all of that?"

Shifora's eyes glistened with a mixture of pain and determination. "I stumbled upon a post on Instagram by Gaur Gopal Das. He spoke about the importance of self-reflection and how it's the foundation for personal growth. It hit me hard.

I realized I had never truly looked back at my life with an honest, critical eye. So, I decided to start."

Sid's brow furrowed in empathy. "That sounds intense. What did you find when you started reflecting?"

A small, bittersweet smile curved Shifora's lips. "I saw a lot of mistakes, missed opportunities, and moments where I had let myself down. But I also saw strength and resilience that I had forgotten about. It was like uncovering a buried treasure of experiences that had shaped me."

Sid leaned in, genuinely interested. "How do you relate this process to the red color of the rainbow?"

Shifora's face lit up with a newfound clarity. "Red is the color of the root chakra, which represents our foundation and sense of security. For me, self-reflection was about going back to my roots, understanding my fears, insecurities, and the core of my being. It was like reigniting the fire within me, a fire that had been smothered by years of neglect."

She paused, her voice steady yet filled with emotion. "As I reflected on the past seven years, I saw the patterns in my decisions and the underlying reasons for my actions. I acknowledged the times I had been too hard on myself and the times I had given up too easily. It was painful, but it was also enlightening."

Sid's eyes softened with understanding. "That sounds powerful. What was the most significant realization you had?"

Shifora looked out the window, lost in thought for a moment. "The most significant realization was that I had been living my life based on others' expectations rather than my own. I had lost touch with what truly made me happy and fulfilled. Self-reflection helped me see that I needed to rebuild my life based on my values and desires."

Sid's expression was one of admiration and respect. "That's incredibly insightful, Shifora. It takes a lot of courage to confront your past like that."

Shifora cheerful, a genuine warmth radiating from her. "It does, but it's worth it. Self-reflection helped me understand that my journey wasn't just about surviving; it was about thriving. It taught me that every experience, no matter how painful, was a step towards becoming the person I am today. And that person is someone I'm learning to love and respect."

Sid leaned back, a thoughtful look on his face. "It's like painting your life with the bold strokes of red, reminding yourself of your passion, your energy, and your right to exist fully and authentically."

Shifora nodded, her eyes shining with gratitude. "Exactly. 'Red' symbolizes the strength and courage I've found within myself. It's a reminder that I have the power to shape my destiny, starting with understanding and accepting who I am at my core, and that was possible only after self-reflection."

Fifty-Three

Orange of Rainbow – Self-Realisation

'Sid couldn't help but tease Shifora. "So, Miss Reflective, what's next on your rainbow journey? Have you discovered the pot of gold yet?"

Shifora cackled, rolling her eyes playfully. "Oh, Sid, if only it were that easy. But yes, the next step after reflection was self-realization."

Sid raised an eyebrow, intrigued. "Self-realization, huh? And how does that fit into your colorful spectrum?"

"Orange," Shifora replied with a smile. "It's the color of the sacral chakra, which represents creativity, passion, and emotional expression. For me, self-realization was about recognizing my true potential and understanding my worth."

Sid leaned forward, his eyes shining, "Alright, color me interested. What did you realize about yourself?"

Shifora's expression turned thoughtful. "I realized that

I had been underestimating myself for a long time. I was always so focused on my flaws and mistakes that I forgot to acknowledge my strengths and achievements. One particular incident stands out."

Sid gestured for her to continue. "Do tell. I'm all ears."

"Not that I am promoting Gaur Gopal Das here, but apparently, in one of the videos that I came across, he was talking about self-worth and how we often seek validation from others when it should come from within. He said something that hit me: 'You are enough just as you are. Your worth is not determined by someone else's opinion of you.'"

Sid's eyes widened in surprise. " That must have been a powerful moment."

Shifora nodded, her eyes reflecting the emotion of that moment. "It was. It was like a light bulb went off in my head. I realized that I had been holding myself back, not because I lacked the ability, but because I lacked the belief in myself. That realization was liberating. It was like the orange color burst into my life, filling it with energy and confidence."

Sid grinned, clearly impressed. "So, you started believing in your potential. How did that change things for you?"

"It changed everything," Shifora said with a smile. "I started focusing on myself. I surrounded myself with people who uplifted me, who saw my worth and reminded me of it when I forgot. I started pursuing activities that made me happy, like writing and singing, which I had abandoned years ago."

Sid's face lit up with admiration. "That's amazing, Shifora. It sounds like self-realization set you on a new path."

"It did," Shifora agreed. "And it wasn't just about hobbies or relationships. It was about recognizing my worth as a person. I realized that I deserved happiness, respect, and love, not because of what I achieved, but because of who I am."

Sid nodded, his expression thoughtful. "So, orange is your color of awakening. It's about realizing you're more than what you've been told or believed about yourself."

Fifty-Four

The Yellow of the Rainbow – Self Acceptance

"Alright, Shifora, we've tackled reflection and realization. What's next on this colorful journey of yours? Are we getting to the pot of gold yet?" Sid with an Impish Shine in his eye.

Shifora snickered, "Patience, Sid. We're just getting to the sunshine – the yellow of self-acceptance."

Sid arched an eyebrow, intrigued. "Self-acceptance, huh? Sounds deep. How did you tie that to yellow?"

Shifora took a sip of her coffee, her expression turning serious. "Yellow is the color of the solar plexus chakra. It represents personal power, confidence, and self-worth. For me, self-acceptance was a crucial part of my journey, especially after feeling so lost for so long. One day I came across a post from a popular motivational account. It said something that resonated deeply with me, you cannot heal what you don't reveal. Accept yourself, and you will find the strength to heal and grow.'"

Sid nodded, absorbing her words. "That's powerful, Shifora. What did you do after reading that?"

Shifora sighed, a small smile playing on her lips. "I realized that I had been fighting against myself for so long, trying to be perfect, trying to meet everyone else's expectations. But I wasn't accepting who I truly was. That night, I decided to embrace my imperfections and accept myself as I am."

Sid's eyes lit up with admiration. "And how did that change

things for you?"

Shifora's expression brightened. "It was like a weight lifted off my shoulders. I started to see myself in a new light. I acknowledged my struggles and my pain, but I also recognized my strengths and my resilience."

Sid grinned, clearly moved by her story. "So, yellow is your color of acceptance. It's about finding the light within, despite the darkness around you."

Fifty-Five

Green of Rainbow – Self Forgiveness

'Sid signaled the café staff for another round of french fries to go along with the coffee, his eyes never leaving Shifora's face. "So, we've talked about self-reflection, self-realization, and self-acceptance. What's next in this colorful journey of yours?"

Shifora radiant. "Green. The color of self-forgiveness."

Sid leaned in, intrigued. "Ah, forgiveness. The hardest yet the most liberating. Tell me, how did you navigate that?"

Shifora took a deep breath, her eyes reflecting a mix of past pain and newfound peace. "Forgiveness was like unclenching a fist I didn't even know I'd been holding for years. I had to forgive myself for so much. For thinking I was responsible for ruining Arif's life. For putting my parents through a series of embarrassments. For being a ruthless colleague. For being an emotionless sibling."

Sid nodded, his gaze steady. "Heavy stuff. What was the

turning point?"

Shifora paused, gathering her thoughts. "I came across a quote by Radhakrishnan Pillai, the author of *Corporate Chanakya*. He wrote, 'The first step towards change is forgiveness. It is through forgiveness that we can leave the past behind and move forward.' It hit me hard. I realized I was carrying these burdens like a badge of honor, but they were only weighing me down."

Sid's eyes twinkled with admiration. "That's powerful. So, you just decided to forgive yourself one day?"

Shifora shook her head. "No, it was a process. I wrote letters to myself. I wrote about the guilt I felt for thinking I had spoiled Arif's life, for the embarrassment I caused my parents, for the way I treated my colleagues, and for the emotional distance I kept from my siblings. I poured it all out, and then I forgave myself in those letters. I told myself it was okay to make mistakes, and that I was human. I rewrote the same stories like how I had wished they should have been, the positive ones, the ones with the happy endings. I burnt the paper and poured the ashes onto the plants."

Sid leaned back, a thoughtful expression on his face. "That's deep. And did it work?"

Shifora nodded, her smile more genuine now. "It did. Slowly but surely. Each time I forgave myself for something, it was like shedding a layer of old, heavy skin. I felt lighter and freer. I began to see myself as deserving of happiness and peace."

Sid raised his coffee cup in a toast. "To self-forgiveness, then. It's a journey worth celebrating."

Shifora clinked her cup against his. "To self-forgiveness. And to move forward without the weight of the past."

Sid's eyes sparkled with mischief. "You know, you should write a book about all this. You've got some viral-worthy insights here."

Shifora laughed, "Maybe one day. For now, I'm content sharing it with a good friend over coffee."

Fifty-Six

Blue of Rainbow – Self-Development

'Sid grinned. "Well, consider me hooked. What's the next color in this rainbow of yours?"

Shifora's smile grew. "Blue. The color of self-development. But that's a story for another cup of coffee."

Sid took a sip of his coffee, his eyes twinkling. "Self-development, huh? That sounds like a chapter filled with action and growth. Tell me more."

Shifora nodded, her eyes lighting up. "It was. After forgiving myself, I felt this immense need to grow and evolve. I started reading more, seeking wisdom from various sources. One of the first books that had a profound impact on me was *Think Like a Monk* by Jay Shetty. His insights on mindfulness and purpose were game-changing."

Sid raised an eyebrow. "Jay Shetty, huh? Interesting.

Shifora paused, reflecting on her journey. "He talked about decluttering the mind, focusing on what's truly important, and living a life of purpose. One quote that stuck with me was, 'Your identity should be made by your virtues, not your valuables.' It made me realize that I needed to shift my focus inward and develop qualities that would make me a better person."

Sid nodded thoughtfully. "So, how did you start putting these ideas into practice?"

Shifora leaned forward, her enthusiasm evident. "Writing down my thoughts was the first step. It helped me track my progress and understand my journey. And I made a conscious effort to socialize more—connecting with people, listening to their stories, and sharing my own experiences. Each conversation gave me a fresh perspective."

Sid chortled. "So, the social butterfly emerged from the cocoon. Is that why you agreed to finally meet me? "

Shifora cackled, "Something like that. I also started exploring new places, and traveling whenever I could. It was like therapy for my soul. Seeing new places, meeting new people, and experiencing different cultures broadened my horizons."

Sid leaned back, clearly impressed. "Sounds like you were on a mission. What else did you do?"

Shifora's smile grew. "I followed motivational speakers like Jay Shetty on social media. His videos were like daily doses of inspiration. One particular video where he said, 'Don't let your actions be driven by fear, let them be driven by love,' really struck a chord with me. It became my mantra."

Sid's eyes twinkled with mischief. "You know, Shifora, if you keep sharing these pearls of wisdom, you might just go viral."

Shifora's eyes sparkled as she continued. "I began with small daily exercises. Meditation, for instance. It helped me center myself and reduce the noise in my mind. I also started journaling, which allowed me to process my thoughts and emotions more clearly."

Fifty-Seven

Indigo of Rainbow – Self-Healing

'Sid leaned back in his chair, his gaze steady on Shifora. "Alright, Shifora, we've journeyed through reflection, realization, acceptance, forgiveness, and development. How did you start mending those deep wounds?"

Shifora took a deep breath, her expression reflecting a blend of vulnerability and strength. "Self-healing was a whole new chapter for me. It was about addressing the internal scars and learning to nurture myself. One of the first things I did was establish a consistent self-care routine. I started incorporating simple practices like aromatherapy and mindfulness into my daily life."

Sid's eyebrows lifted proudly. "Aromatherapy? How did that help?"

Shifora's eyes softened. "I discovered that essential oils could have a calming effect on my mind. Lavender and chamomile became my go-to scents. I'd light a candle and let the soothing aromas fill my space. It was like creating a sanctuary within my own home."

Sid nodded, clearly intrigued. "And what about mindfulness? How did that fit into your healing process?"

Shifora's smile was gentle. "Mindfulness taught me to stay present and observe my thoughts without judgment. I practiced it through guided meditations and mindful breathing exercises. It was a way to detach from the chaos and find stillness amidst the storm."

Sid leaned forward, his curiosity evident. "Did you try anything else to aid in your healing?"

Shifora's expression became thoughtful. "Yes, I began exploring creative outlets. Painting, for instance, became a form of therapy. I found that expressing myself through art allowed me to process emotions that words couldn't capture. My origami was filled with colors and textures that reflected my inner world."

Sid's eyes widened with admiration. "That's beautiful. How did art contribute to your healing journey?"

Shifora's gaze became distant as if recalling the experience. "Each craft was a way to release pent-up feelings. I didn't focus on creating something perfect, instead, I let my emotions guide the process. It was a form of self-expression and catharsis."

Sid's tone was encouraging. "And what about physical activities? Did you incorporate any into your routine?"

Shifora nodded vigorously. "Absolutely. Yoga became a cornerstone of my healing journey. It helped me reconnect with my body and release built-up tension. Through yoga, I learned to honor my physical self and appreciate its strength and resilience."

Sid giggled lightly. "Yoga and aromatherapy sounds like you

were building your little haven."

"Exactly. Journaling helped me shift my focus from what I'd lost to what I still had, and that made a significant difference in my outlook." Shifora saif softly.

Sid leaned back, his tone playful. "So, any more colors in this rainbow of yours?"

Shifora's eyes sparkled with mischief. "Yes, the last color is violet, the color of inner peace."

Fifty-Eight

Violet of Rainbow – Self Love

"Have you ever dated yourself?" Shifora asked Sid, a playful glint in her eye.

Sid looked at Shifora in surprise. "What? Dated myself?"

"Yes," Shifora said, leaning in with a smile. "You know, taking yourself out, treating yourself with the same love and care you would for a partner."

"Well, I guess I've never thought about it that way. How does one go about dating oneself?" Sid Doubted.

Shifora's expression turned thoughtful. " What I realized is that the love I sought from Arif was something I had failed to cultivate within myself. I was striving to be what they wanted to see in me, but as we know, superficial things don't endure. I was searching for the love I felt deprived of, yet I hadn't even loved myself in the way I desired others to love me. As *The Secret* puts it, "You attract what you are, not what you want."

True, lasting love begins within. By embracing and loving ourselves, we naturally attract the genuine love we seek from others."

"I like it when you said that, that's deep. I never thought about that. Sid Admitted. "How did you express your love then?"

"It started with small acts of kindness towards myself. For instance, I remember one evening, I decided to take myself out to my favorite café. Shifora continued, "One thing I did was create a daily ritual. Every morning, I'd look in the mirror and say something positive to myself. It felt silly at first, but over time, it made a difference. It was like I was reprogramming my brain to focus on the good."

"Did you use any particular resources or inspirations?" Sid asked.

"Yes, I found inspiration from various sources," Shifora said. "One quote that stuck with me was from Tony Robbins, 'The quality of your life is the quality of your relationships, including the one you have with yourself.' It made me realize that if I wanted to improve my life, I needed to start with how I treated myself."

Sid swayed back, absorbing her words. "So, what else did you do to nurture self-love?"

"I started exploring new hobbies and interests," Shifora said. "I took up swimming, something I'd always wanted to try but never did. It became a form of therapy, a way to express my emotions and connect with myself on a deeper level."

"Did you find it difficult to maintain this practice?" Sid asked.

"At times, yes," Shifora admitted. "There were days when self-doubt would creep in, and I'd question my worth. But I reminded myself that self-love is a journey, not a destination. It's about progress, not perfection. Whenever I stumbled, I'd pick myself up and keep going. But I reminded myself of what my friend Once said "The day you don't feel like doing it, is the day you need it" Now you can relate or apply this sentence wherever you wish, it works!!."

Shifora paused, her eyes reflecting the violet hues of the rainbow she described. "So I applied Violet from Rainbow to self-love, because it symbolizes spirituality and inner peace. It's about finding harmony within yourself and embracing who you are, flaws and all. By nurturing love for myself, I created a sense of inner calm and strength that allowed me to face life's challenges with grace."

Sid listened, his expression thoughtful as he absorbed Shifora's words. After a pause, he gave a small, playful shrug. "Alright, I'll admit, all this rainbow and 'shades of healing' talk has me thinking deeply. But don't expect me to start journaling or swapping stories at the nearest support group anytime soon." He shot her a lopsided grin. "I mean, I'm still Sid—at best, you'll catch me testing my own 'shade' by surviving my next existential crisis over a coffee."

"Baby steps, Sid. You can even have a shade or two." Shifora justified.

"Only if it comes with a disclaimer," he said, smirking. "Self-reflection without Sid-ification? Not happening."

Fifty-Nine

Under the Evening Sky

'By now, darkness had enveloped the café where Sid and Shifora sat, nearly finishing their rounds of coffee. Shifora moved forward, Intrigue awakened, "So, Sid, this is all about me now, It feels like an open book."

Sid paused, contemplating his response before admitting, "Honestly, before meeting you today, I had different feelings about you. But now, I have immense respect for you. You've stood by yourself, and that's what matters most.

"I can go on and on," Sid continued, but he glanced at his watch and the darkening sky outside. Despite his reluctance for Shifora to leave, he added with a hint of hesitation, "It might be getting late for you. I'll walk you halfway home."

Shifora wanted to hear more from Sid, but hesitated, unsure of how he might perceive her feelings now, after rejecting him multiple times. She agreed with a nod and strolled towards her apartment.

As they walked along the dimly lit streets of Malé, a soft breeze carried the scent of evening jasmine, adding a touch of romance to the air. The city lights cast a gentle glow on their faces, highlighting the unspoken connection between Sid and Shifora. In the quiet between their words, their eyes met with a silent understanding, each step forward seemed to draw them closer emotionally. Sid broke the silence.

"What keeps you busy nowadays?" Sid broke the silence.

I kept myself busier than a squirrel stashing acorns. I'm never idle, I find idle too idling, you know?" She winked, a hint of mischief in her eyes."Meeting so many inspiring souls in my life made me realize it was time to pay it forward. So, I birthed 1st Inning, a mental health support where we talk, be there for each other, support, offer remedies, and therapies, and help overcome and evolve, with I try to help many of those who need inspiration.

"Wow, that's impressive! A mental health organization… You're truly beyond what I ever imagined, Shifora," Sid expressed, admiration evident in his voice.

As they reached the corner where they would part ways, Sid paused, hesitating for a moment. He looked at Shifora, his eyes reflecting the moonlight above. "You know, Shifora," he began softly. "Tonight has been unexpectedly wonderful."

Shifora touched by his sincerity. The evening had indeed been surprisingly pleasant, and Sid's company had been a soothing balm to her soul. She blushed.

Sid took a step closer, his gaze locking with hers. "Maybe we could do this again sometime," he suggested, his tone hopeful yet respectful of her boundaries. "Unless you disappear again".

Shifora glanced at Sid with a slight smile. "Hey, do you wanna sit for a bit?" she asked, nodding towards the bench overlooking the beach just outside her apartment building.

Sid nodded eagerly, though he masked his enthusiasm with a calm demeanor. "Of course," he replied, hoping to prolong their time together.

Under the soft moonlight, the beach stretched out before them, the waves rhythmically kissing the shore. The air was cool and carried the salty tang of the sea, while the distant stars sparkled like scattered diamonds in the night sky. The moon casts a gentle glow, adding a touch of magic to their surroundings.

As they settled on the bench, Sid couldn't help but steal glances at Shifora, admiring her profile against the serene backdrop. "So, what have you thought about the future?" Sid finally asked, trying to gauge Shifora's thoughts.

Shifora paused for a moment, gazing out at the tranquil sea. "I've just discovered myself," she began, her voice carrying a sense of newfound clarity. "I've learned how to enjoy my own company. I think I need this time with myself now."

Sid listened intently, sensing the weight of her words. " I think it was all planned by the Universe. More than me the supreme power knew that returning to Maldives was essential for my self-reflection, for self-forgiveness, and ultimately, for healing," Shifora continued, her voice tinged with introspection. "I've realized over these seven years here that what I was seeking all along was healing and I learned it off lately, and I assume that was the right time. It's surprising how our priorities shift.

Sid nodded thoughtfully, intrigued by her journey. "What does that mean?" he probed gently, wanting to understand more.

"It means I'm going back to my native," Shifora replied.

"I want to help others who may be going through similar struggles. It's a struggle of first identifying self, accepting it, forgiving it."

"What? We have just met. Are you talking about disappearing again?" Sid questioned, his heart swelling with a touch of sadness. But thought to himself *"Her journey had been long and arduous, and her commitment to helping others was a testament to her strength and resilience."*

Yet, amid this moment of discovery, Sid felt an undeniable urge to address the lingering question that had haunted him for years.

"Shifora, I want to know more about you, what happened after college? Where did you disappear to? And what about your dream of joining the army?" Sid bombarded her with questions, clearly eager to prolong the conversation.

Shifora replied with a smile, "Well, for that, you'll have to come to Goa. We can talk about it there."

The moonlight cast a soft glow on their faces as they walked in silence, the weight of unspoken words hanging between them. Sid's mind raced, memories of their shared past flashing before his eyes. The laughter, the camaraderie, the unfulfilled promises, all of it culminated in this moment.

Taking a deep breath, Sid stopped and turned to face Shifora. His eyes bore into hers with a mixture of hope and determination. "Shifora," he began, his voice steady but filled with emotion, "Would you like to think again about the question I asked you decades ago?"

Shifora looked at Sid, her eyes widening in surprise. The intensity of his gaze, the sincerity in his voice, it was as if time had stood still, and they were back to that pivotal moment in their youth.

Sid took a step closer, his hand reaching out to gently touch hers. "I promise you," he said softly, "I will love you more than I ever did. Mujhe tumhara haath mil sakta hai? (Can I marry you)?"

Before Shifora could respond, "Shifora!" a familiar voice called out with a mix of warmth and excitement.

Sid's heart skipped a beat as he turned to see a tall, well-built man striding toward them. His confidence was undeniable as if he belonged in every frame of this moment. Before Shifora could even react, Neil wrapped his arms around her in a tight embrace, lifting her slightly off the ground, his laughter echoing into the quiet night.

"I've missed you!" Neil's voice was full of casual familiarity, and Sid's chest tightened.

Shifora, taken by surprise, giggled softly, playfully swatting Neil's shoulder as she caught her breath. "Neil! I didn't expect to see you here."

Sid watched, his mind racing. Who was this guy? Was there something going on between them? He masked his confusion with a faint smile, but his thoughts were anything but calm.

Neil finally released Shifora, his eyes twinkling as he glanced at Sid. "Oh, hey. I didn't mean to interrupt anything." He flashed a quick grin, but something about his demeanor made Sid feel as though the interruption was very much intentional.

"Sid, this is Neil. We've known each other for years," Shifora explained casually, though Sid couldn't help but notice the way Neil lingered just a little too close to her.

"Nice to meet you," Sid said, offering a handshake, though his mind was already questioning everything, *"who exactly was Neil to Shifora?"*

The night stretched on, the waves crashing in the distance

echoing his turbulent thoughts. As he watched them, questions swirled in his mind: Could he let her go again? Was there still a chance for them? Or had Neil stepped in to fill a void he hadn't even known existed?

Whatever happened next, he knew one thing, the journey ahead was bound to be filled with twists and turns. Would he have the courage to confront his feelings, or would he find himself watching from the sidelines once more?

Sid was left standing there, unsure of what to think, but knowing one thing for certain, their story wasn't over yet.

* * *

Sixty

Conclusion

As Shifora closes this chapter of her life, she reminds us all of an essential truth, healing isn't linear, and self-acceptance isn't a destination, it's a journey. In a world that often demands perfection and thrives on comparison, this story is a gentle nudge to step away from the noise and embrace our imperfect, authentic selves. It's about finding the courage to love who we are, not despite our scars, but because of them.

As you turn the final page, may this book serve as a companion in your own healing journey, a reminder that your story matters, and that every step forward, no matter how small, is a victory worth celebrating. The race was never about who finishes first, it's about running it your way, at your own pace, with your heart wide open.

Stay tuned! Follow for updates on the release of the sequel to *7 Shades of Healing,* and if you'd love to explore Shifora's beginnings in a prequel, reach out to the author, your voice could inspire the next chapter!

Epilogue

Shifora stood at the edge of the cliff, her arms spread wide as the breeze carried the scent of the sea. The sun dipped low on the horizon, painting the sky in hues of orange and gold a reminder that endings, no matter how bittersweet, hold the promise of a new dawn.

For years, she had carried the weight of her past, mistakes, regrets, and the unspoken fear of never being enough. But as the tides below crashed against the rocks, she realized that life wasn't about erasing those scars. It was about learning to live with them, letting them become a testament to her resilience.

She thought about the people who had shaped her journey, those who had loved her, those who had hurt her, and those who had simply been passing chapters in her story. Each one had played a role, teaching her lessons she hadn't understood until now. She no longer sought closure from them; instead, she found it within herself.

In that moment, she whispered a silent thank you to her past. It had broken her, yes, but it had also rebuilt her into someone stronger, someone softer, someone who could finally look in the mirror and say, "I love you" without hesitation.

As Shifora turned to leave, her heart felt light, lighter than it had in years. She didn't know what the future held, but she no longer feared it. For the first time, she felt free. Free to love, free to forgive, and free to live for herself.

This wasn't the end of her story. It was just the beginning of a new chapter, one she would write with her head held high and her heart wide open. And for anyone reading this, she left one final message:

"No matter where you are in your journey, remember this—you are worthy of healing, of love, and of joy. And no matter how broken you feel, you will rise again. Just like I did." .... *Algira Pereira*

Afterword

As I write this, I am filled with gratitude for you, dear reader, for choosing to accompany Shifora on her journey of self-healing, self-forgiveness, and growth. *7 Shades of Healing* is more than just a story; it is a reflection of struggles we all face, a reminder that healing is not linear, and a testament to the strength we carry within us, even when we feel most broken.

This book was written with the hope that it would inspire you to pause, reflect, and embrace the unique beauty of your own journey. Life is messy, unpredictable, and at times overwhelming—but it is also breathtakingly beautiful when we learn to live it on our own terms, with love and compassion for ourselves.

If Shifora's story resonated with you, know that you are not alone. If it sparked emotions you didn't realize you had, I hope it also brought you closer to understanding and accepting yourself.

This isn't the end, Shifora's journey continues, and I am thrilled to share that a **sequel** is in the works! Stay tuned for more of her story as she navigates new challenges and uncovers new layers of healing.

And if you'd like to explore how it all began, I'd love to hear from you. A prequel could bring Shifora's past to life with your encouragement and support!

To my readers, thank you for being a part of this journey. Your love and feedback mean the world to me. Healing may not come overnight, but together, we can inspire each other to take the first step toward a brighter, more fulfilling life.

With love and gratitude,

Algira Pereira

About the Author

Algira Pereira is a hospitality professional from Goa, India, with an MBA in Business Management. Though she grew up dreaming of joining the defence forces, life's winds carried her into the dynamic world of hospitality. Algira makes her writing debut with *7 Shades of Healing*, a book that reflects her passion for helping others on their mental health journeys. Outside of writing, you'll find her planning, organizing, and indulging in her love for creativity.

You can connect with me on:

🌐 https://www.linkedin.com/in/algirapereira

🔗 https://www.instagram.com/algira_pereira/profilecard/?igsh=aXhneXpoeXdtNGtl

9 7 9 8 8 9 6 7 3 1 2 0 7